Blue Dragon Fantasy;
Faded Memories and Short Stories

Ryan Keith Johnson

ISBN   978-0-615-83630-0

Copy Right © 2015, © 2020 by Ryan Keith Johnson,
All rights reserved.
Produced by Red and Blue Dragon Fantasy LLC.
Cover Design by Ryan Keith Johnson

Other Titles:

The King's Retribution (2007)
What I Think About You; Song Lyrics and Poetry (2011)
Lion Ascend (2011)
The Temple of the Incubus (2011)
Blue Dragon Fantasy; Faded Memories and Short Stories (2015)
Red Dragon Fantasy; Song Lyrics and Poetry (2019)
The Culminate Amethyst (2019)
An Angel's Whisper (2019)

Table of contents

<u>Closer; Faded Memories Do Become Real</u>

It was a day that Cynthia Wise would never forget. She ran through the hallways of the hospital after receiving a call from the State Patrol. Her fiancé was involved in a head on collision with a semi. She was stopped at the emergency room by the doctor that was in charge and dropped her purse after hearing what he said. The possessions fell on the floor from her unzipped bag. Cynthia kneeled down to pick up her things and began to tremble with the thought that Jericho would be a vegetable for the rest of his life. The feelings persisted until she walked into his room to see him sleeping. She kneeled down next to him on his bed slowly.

"Your dreaming now," began Cynthia while running her fingers through his thick sandy brown hair. "When you wake we will leave this behind as a faded memory," she smiled while looking at him with her green eyes and ran her fingers through his hair. He looked the same as he did a year ago when she met him on her seventeenth birthday. They were together in the hospital room and it was late.

Cynthia would have to leave, but remembered her own accident when she was seventeen. She turned her wrist as the memory unfolded; the car accident followed with the tow truck taking the car away. She was laid up in the hospital for weeks but it was a blessing because it allowed her and Jericho to become closer. The scar was shaped like a rose and was a sign from God to continue living. Cynthia left the hospital and called it a night.

The next day the loneliness continued to penetrate Cynthia and she decided to visit Jericho. She walked into the room and untied her long, curly, cinnamon color hair to look at her fiancé who was awake. He looked the same as before, but with a little more color in his high cheek bones. His blue eyes widened as he looked at her.

"How are you feeling?" she asked with a smile.
"Fine, I think," replied Jericho. "Who are you?"

The words stabbed Cynthia like a knife driven in her heart. She didn't expect
Jericho to get amnesia and began to snivel, while walking towards him, "I'm your future
wife."
The young man touched his head and then moved his hand out to show that he

3

wanted her to keep away. The bandage on his forehead and police reports proved that he
hit his head hard against the wind shield.

"I think I would remember proposing to you and I don't," began Jericho.

"But I am," Cynthia replied.

"Then what's my favorite color?" he demanded.

"Blue."

"What's my favorite cartoon character?"

"Mickey Mouse," she answered

"What is my favorite movie?"

"Gone In Sixty Seconds," she continued.

His eyes widened with surprise and the question remained; how did this person
know all this? This stranger who said he was about to marry her, could not possibly know
everything.

"What cologne do I wear?" Jericho continued as he heard Cynthia let out a sigh.

"I'm not going to play twenty questions with you, I'm telling you the truth."

Just then a nurse stepped into the room with a clip board and a cart with medical
devices. The nurse looked like an ordinary middle aged woman dressed in white and she looked at Cynthia with concern. Jericho let out a sigh of relief, glad that someone was there to keep watch. He didnt' trust Cynthia because she was a stranger to him and knew everything about him.

"Ms. Wise, I need to do a medical examination. Could you please leave the
room?" asked the nurse.

"I'll come back tomorrow," replied Cynthia as she looked at Jericho.

Cynthia sat on the couch in her apartment that she shared with Jericho and opened a small pale of ice cream. She had taken the week off from her receptionist job, working for her dad, and was keeping herself occupied so Jericho wouldn't push her away. She closed her eyes and remembered her car accident. Her eyes welled up with tears as the faded memories emerged and she started crying.

"How are you doing today?" asked Jericho as he looked into her eyes.

"Better than yesterday," Cynthia answered as she scratched the scab onher wrist.

"You know you should stop that or it will turn into a scar," replied Jericho.

"I don't care, it itches," she replied and heard Jericho laugh.

"You've got a stubborn heart, more than I could imagine."

The weeks progressed and before long they were living their life again. Jericho walked through the park and turned Cynthia's wrist over to see the scar of the upside down rose. It was vivid and questions were asked, but one question seemed to pop in his mind; how did she survive the accident?

They stood near a swing set and he picked Cynthia up and sat her on a tree stump. They could feel each other's heartbeat and began kissing. Cynthia didn't want it to end and knew that Jericho didn't want it to end either.

"That's an interesting tattoo you have there," he whispered.
"Oh yeah I know," she answered while looking at the rose and then into
her boyfriend's eyes. "I guess it's my destiny to get a second chance. Faded memories do
become real."
"Yes, I guess you could say that a lot of things become real and when I
met you on your birthday I wanted to ask you this question?" replied Jericho as
he got down on one knee and pulled out a small box.

Cynthia felt a dizzy wave of excitement that swept her insides with the
feeling of butterflies. She could feel the hair on the back of her neck stand on end;
the feeling of an electric current shot up and down her spine as she touched the
box. She smiled emerged and tried to keep from crying out of excitement.

"Cynthia Wise, I don't want to put any pressure on you and I've waited a
year," replied Jericho as he opened the black box to reveal a wedding ring.
"Will you marry me?" he asked and after a slight hesitation he got his answer.
"Yes" she answered with a laugh and kissed him.

Cynthia stopped crying and wiped her tears as she smiled from the flashback; it was nice to remember the things that were memorable. She wished for that feeling of love instead of being lonely. The eighteen year old got up from the couch and walked up to turn the television off when she began thinking about the inevitable. How was she to help Jericho remember her she thought and realized if she did nothing the relationship would be gone.

Tomorrow would be a new start to get him back she thought to herself. She would get close to him, but there was a need to be careful. Trying to help Jericho would be like trying to help a wounded tiger. Cynthia turned the light off and went to bed.

The next day at the hospital, Cynthia walked into Jericho's room with a tray of food and saw him picking his wound. She smiled as she walked over and set the tray of food on the bed's swing board to set food on. He smiled, but the smile was a façade and she could tell he didn't trust her.

"You know if you keep picking your scab it's going to turn into a scar."

"I don't care, it itches," he answered as he grabbed the apple from the tray and took a bite. Cynthia smiled and began to laugh.

"What's so funny?" he asked.

"Nothing," began Cynthia. "You know in a couple days you might be well enough to leave the hospital."

"In a couple days you may want a different boyfriend," replied Jericho as he watched Cynthia look at him with concern.

"I was hoping that you would allow me to help you with your rehabilitation to remember things," said Cynthia.

"I don't know," began Jericho. "I think I'm a lost cause, I'm screwed up you know. You're an attractive woman who deserves someone who hasn't smashed up his brain."

"Let's give it time," she replied. "I'm not going anywhere."

As the days progressed and turned to weeks; Jericho worked hard to re-learn how to walk. He worked hard and struggled in the excersizes but succeeded in the end. After a couple more days he was able to leave and the former lovers walked around the park and had some small talk. Cynthia walked with him with a photo album to help him remember family and friends. She touched his hand as she watched him smile and nod his head as he looked less confused and more confident. It was slowly coming back, but the remaining puzzle piece was still not in place.

It was Sunday afternoon and Cynthia earned his trust and was holding his hand. They had come so far since the accident that it was magical. Cynthia felt they had become close and as they walked through a familiar part of the park she felt a cold empty feeling. She was scared that he wasn't going to remember this special place.

Would it be possible that he would remember her and special memories they shared? They stopped near a swing set and she sat on the tree stump to look into his eyes.

"Do you remember this place?" asked Cynthia as she licked her lips.

"It feels familiar, but I can't place it. Maybe you should explain why it's so paramount?"

"Right here, on this same sunny day, you asked me to marry you."

Cynthia smiled as the memories emerged in her mind; it slowly subsided to expressing anxiety while clouded mystery of *what ifs* and *how could this be* became apparent. It looked like Jericho was turning away and she expressed fear that she would lose her soulmate forever. Her legs were numb and she sat town on the tree stump to relax. Jericho looked around and felt the wind brush up against his face as he realized the whole area was reminesent. He couldn't put his finger on it, yet it all made sense to him somehow and he turned his head to look at Cynthia and she looked at him waiting for what he had to say.

There was a moment of silence as Jericho stared into Cynthia's green eyes while pictures fluttered in his mind. He suddenly remembered a voice that was like hers as well as the laughter and kisses, dancing in the rain, feeding each other ice cream. Then suddenly there was the sound of words that rang in his mind and echoed his ears; that faded memories do become real.

"I don't want to add any pressure on you, but you're hurting me," she answered and started to cry with light sniffles as her lips began to tremble, but she held herself together while her eyes welled with tears.

"This relationship can go two ways; one way is you trust me and let me in. The other, is we go our separate ways and never see each other again."

"If I was able to fall in love with you then give me chance to fall in love with you again," replied Jericho adamantly.

"I can't," cried Cynthia as she got up from the stump and turned away, but Jericho walked over to her, grabbed her shoulders and turned her around to look in her eyes. He touched her face gently with his hand and move in as though he was about to kiss her, but he stopped.

"I can't face this isolation," began Cynthia emotionally. "Or hope that one day you'll remember me when I feel like it's never going to happen. You have your life and I have mine," Cynthia cried and she broke free from his grip and walked away.

Jericho's mouth dropped and tears emerged, but didn't drop because he wiped them with his hand. The memories rushed through his mind like water, busting through a dam.

He remembered and it stuck into his mind like a tac, she had fallen on some ice in January a few years back on her birthday and needed help getting home because her car wouldn't start.

Jericho helped her off the ice and offered to give her a ride home. The next morning he fixed her car and drove it to her house. She was happy and made him breakfast, they quickly became friends and went on their first date to her sister's dance recital. Then they kept bumping into each other at malls, school and parks. He continued to ask her out and they became a couple that were envied by many people at high school.

Jericho grabbed her wrist and saw the upside down rose, which sent chills up his spine because he suddenly remembered how she got it. Cynthia turned her head and realized that he didn't want her to go. It was the same look that she saw when they danced at Prom.

"Faded memories do become real," he declared as he held her close, closer than she had been held in a time that seemed to be eternity.

Cynthia looked down, past his shorts to his knee cap where he had been caught scratching the scar that she told him repeatedly to stop and saw a scar of an upside down rose. It was a sign that they were meant for each other and that they would never lose each other again.

"I missed you," she whispered as they both left the park realizing they would be together forever.

The Flesh Beast

The cold wet taping of rain scared little Adam as it rang in his ears like bells, but not as much as the lightning that struck by the window with the thunder that followed. It was his first week in the Insane Asylum Correctional Facility for Boys and Girls in the City of Cascade Falls.

The asylum was set up for troubled youngsters who had problems dealing with their feelings. For Adam it was a choice made by his parents who decided it was time for him to grow up and forget about his beliefs in fantasies.

He was only eight years old and on the first day he heard rumors that the institute had a beast that ate children. It came out at night and whispered, where's my flesh? There were no screams to wake up the other children so nothing could be done to save them from this creature known as the Flesh Beast.

The Flesh Beast was a creature from the underworld that lived with its own race. It took turns with its kin to eat naughty children that were disobedient. The children didn't know that the flesh beasts were called by real names and were nothing more than filling in the role as the Flesh Beast.

Adam couldn't sleep; his innocent, green eyes were sapped with tears and every time they closed he could hear the beast whispering, where' s my flesh? Adam remembered exploring the asylum, which was like a castle and felt he was being watched. He had not played hide and seek on his first day until he met Joey and Jennifer, who played the game all the time.

Joey, the black haired boy with brown eyes, was sent to the asylum for throwing rocks at people and stealing candy from little girls. Jennifer, the green eyed, red head, was in the institute for stealing toys from merchant shops and throwing a dog dong at a teacher. Jennifer got ten strikes across her fingers on the first day for calling Ms. Knealson a decrepit old hag.

Adam rose out of bed after hearing something outside his room. He shared the room with Joey who slept above him on the bunk bed. It seemed like every child had committed a crime and all Adam did was believe in unicorns, fairies and all the good things in the world.

"Adam, I hear something," whispered Joey.

Adam was quiet and wondered what Joey heard. Adam didn't have to wait long to hear it and when he did, the hair on his arms stood up. Sweat began to perspire on his cheeks and his ears began to ring as he heard the dreaded question that frightened him.

"Where's my flesh?" it whispered.

Joey's eyes were wide as they both jumped out of bed. The floor creaked with every step the two boys made towards the door and opened it to who it was. The door screetched open from the rusty old hinges.

"Let's go back to our beds," shivered Adam.
"Are you scared?" asked Joey.
 "No, of course not," answered Adam.

The two kids moved outside the door and looked around. They slowly walked down the hallway and they could see shadows in the hallway from the curtains. The wind blew through the open large windows that allowed the moon to shine through with shades of blue.

"I heard stories that the flesh beast tears the muscles from the bones and uses your fingers as tooth picks," whispered Joey.

"Where's my flesh?" it whispered.

Both boys looked at each other scared and then looked ahead in the hallway to see something scary ahead of them in the form of a shadow. The shadow was about twenty-five feet ahead of them with a rob on and what looked like long hair. Suddenly, it started to walk to wards them and the boys held each other scared as it moved its head in veiw for them to see its horrid face.

"Boo!"

The boys jumped with a scream and watched Jennifer emerge into the moon light. She was laughing at them hysterically for being scared of a girl. It seemed to Adam that he wouldn't see the end of being bullied and would be known throughout the asylum as the girly boy.

"You should have seen the look on your guys' face. It was hillarious," she laughed with the snort of a piglet.

"That wasn't funny, there is a flesh beast that kills children. Why woud you impersonate something so evil?" asked Adam. "It wasn't funny."

"It was funny to me," laughed Jennifer. "I got to watch you two huddle together like scared little girls."

"If anybody should get their skin ripped off its you," said Joey as he raised his voice.

"Quiet Joey," whispered Adam. "You'll wake up Ms. Knealson."

"Scaredee cats," snorted Jennifer.

"Where's my flesh?" whispered a raspy voice, but this time it sounded deep and distinct.

A deep growl could be heard that sounded like a wolf or a lion. It was so disturbing that it made all three kids quiet and scared as they honed in on where it came from.

"What was that?" asked Jennifer adamantly, realizing that this wasn't a joking matter.

"I don't know," said Adam.

"I'm going to find out," whispered Joey as he slowly walked down the hallway and Jennifer walked with him.

"Joey," said Adam as he grabed both of them. "Don't do this."

Sweat filled Adam's pores as he heard the dreaded whisper again. He turned around to squint in the darkness and saw a pair of yellow eyes open up. They were glowing and staring back at him, in an evil way. It took a step towards them and the children could tell right away that it wasn't human. It was tall and had a tail, similar to an alligator tail.

"Where's my flesh?" It whispered as the children came closer.

Suddenly, there was an out burst and the creature lunged it's head out in the moonlight and unleashed a bellow, "where's my flesh!"

The loud shriek filled the hallways as Jennifer let out a scream and was about to run away. She could think of nothing better to do than hide under the covers to escape and be in her safe place.

The monster snapped its jaws like an alligator to reveal to reveal its teeth. When it's mouth was open the teeth moved along the jawbone similar to a chainsaw.

"Run back to your room!" Joey screamed as he retreated with the other two children.

Joey turned his head and screamed as loud as he could when something grabbed his ankle with its sharp talons and thrust him on his back to show the boy his wicked smile. It kneeled down to his face as saliva dripped from its teeth.

"You're my flesh!" growled the flesh beast as it swung its claws into the Joey's chest. After Joey screamed and died, the flesh beast feasted upon the boy's corpse. The monster watched Jennifer and Adam run away. It took another bite and chased after the two kids quickly with a growl. It ran after Jennifer like a wolf and roared, "where's my flesh?"

"Run!" she screamed just before the flesh beast pulled her back with the end of its claws embedded in her shoulder and ripped her head off with its teeth. The creature spit out her head and it rolled along the floor like a ball. The flesh beast quickly ripped out her spine and ate her flesh and bone.

Adam started crying and screamed when he saw Jennifer's decapitated head roll on the floor. The boy ran as fast as he could and didn't look back. He knew that the flesh beast was after him and there was no place to hide.

The flesh beast ate the last of Jennifer and persued Adam on all fours. It opened its mouth to reveal its teeth to take its last bite.

Adam made it into his room and slammed the door shut just before the creature could get in. He looked around scared and tried to figure out where he could hide.

"Where is my flesh?" yelled the creature as it leaned up against the door and scratched the surface with its talons.

"Where's my flesh!" the beast growled as it slowly backed away and then charged quickly like a bull. The door busted down and pieces of wood laid splintered on the floor. It looked around for Adam but couldn't find him. The beast could smell urine under the bed and it bent its knees to look under it, but there was nobody there. Drool dripped from its mouth as it rose back up again and looked to the closet.

Adam looked through little whicker material in a secret spot and was shivering. He was so scared, he was so scared that he peed in his pajamas.

"Where's my flesh?" roared the flesh beast like a broken record.

The flesh beast opened the closet door that was open by a crack and looked inside. The closet had clothes hung up and boxes of board games inside as well. The creature smelled area with its long, reptilian muzzle and yellow colored, snake eyes. It couldn't find the boy and suddenly it heard something summon it out of the room.

After a few minutes of silence, Adam popped his head up from the hamper and felt cold and sticky in his wet underpants. He took off his pajamas and threw them aside and put on a clean pair from the dresser. He walked over to the edge of the opening where the broken door was and looked around in the darkness and saw nothing, Suddenly, a wrinkled old hand reached over his mouth with a tissue paper. Adam screamed and squrimed as he felt himself being picked up.

Adam screamed and rose out of bed as he gasped, realizing it was just a nightmare. He got out of bed to see the broken door was fine and when he got out of bed he couldn't find any broken pieces of wood on the floor. His wet pajamas were missing and so was Joey.

Adam couldn't understand it, was it just a nightmare? Maybe it was nightmare and Joey was downstairs eating. Adam picked out his clothes from his dresser to take a bath. After his bath, he went down stairs to eat breakfast.

He sat in his chair in the commons where there were hundreds of children in his age group. He gripped his fork and knife ready to eat, but was still thinking about his nightmare. Ms. Knealson was looking at him as she handed out the plates filled with breakfast and when she got to him she set Adam's plate down before him. Adam opened the cover and screamed at the sight of flesh, two hearts and a pair of eyeballs on some pancakes.

The boy left screaming and running while holding his mouth shut with his hands. Ms. Knealson looked at the plate of eggs, bacon, and pancakes with two slabs of butter on top and then at the running boy and smiled to reveal her her pointy teeth. Her eyes twinkled yellow as she walked to the waste basket and dumped the plate of food.

She sneered while looking at the other children and whispered, "there are still plenty of naughty children that I can feed my pet instead of worrying about the one that escaped."

The creepy woman turned away from the garbage and walked past tables of children and into the kitchen where she could hear the constant whispers, *where's my flesh?*

Fire Starter

Gary August stared outside the window to see the dead grass, sleeping trees and the sunrise. There was a collage of colors that was pink, red, violet and it represented death to him. It was a morning like no other and for Gary it was going to be a day he wouldn't forget.

He scratched his scruffy chin with his finger. His grey eyes revealed that he was fidgity, angry and hadn't gotten any sleep for days. His black hair drooped over his eyes and ears as he noticed a few snowflakes fall next to his window. It was April and the snow had melted on the lawn, but it was starting to snow.

Tears emerged in his eyes as he heard the voices in his head telling him to kill the ones that taunted him. He remembered how they embarrassed, beat him up and laughed at him when he would make mistakes or ask stupid questions in class, but that was a long time ago and now he was a grown up and would have to act mature and natural at his new job at the post office.

They changed him into this carnage of hate. This hate machine that loved to kill people and use guns and knives to shed blood. It was like a lovely green meadow that had become a victim to a wild fire. His classmates teased and hurt him was the wildfire that destroyed his innocence, the child of the past. The teachers and guidance councilors thought he lost his mind and went crazy when he went to high school. The innocence was transformed into vengeance by starting fires to the bullies responsible. It would sometimes start with a bullet in the brain or a knife in the chest, but he never got caught by the police. Even the best detectives in the world could track his trail in the sewers because of the urine and shit they would have to sniff out like hounds. They couldn't find him.

Gary inhaled his cigarette as the window fogged up with the memories unraveled through his mind and became more than real, they haunted him. He loved his Camels and Marlboros and remembered every morning getting ready for school only to be laughed at, mocked and betrayed by those that claimed to be his friend. The so called friends were nothing more than traitors.

Every step of the way, from grade school, junior high to high school of Ever Grove High was nothing but Hell. It was disgusting, but there was nothing he could do about it.

He learned that the real people responsible were the people at the top. They were the ones who called the shots and said what laws would pass, who would pay taxes, who would be allowed to run their business. Gary would have them in his sights and shoot them a bullet in the brain.

"I didn't deserve the crap that I got. I never caused anyone harm nor did I torture anyone the way you did," he said with a rough voice as his hands began to shake like a crack addict as he continued. "Just because I'm different doesn't give anyone the right to persecute me."

His cold empty hand reached for the combination lock as he twisted and turned it. He turned his head to see the girl of his dreams, Julie. He loved the way she parted her long brown hair and the way her brown eyes looked at him. When she spoke, her words served as music in itself. He loved the way her thin lips gestured each syllable when she talked to her friends.

Gary walked over to her, his heart pumping faster with each step as he smiled. Julie turned her eyes and head as he moved towards her. Their eyes locked into each other like a thread of yarn wrapped around their waist.

"Hi," he smiled.

"Oh hi Gary," she answered while pulling out her math book.

Gary had heard that she broke up with her boyfriend and wanted to ask her out. He stopped to think and wondered if he was making a wise choice, would it be ok with the hierarchy of jocks, the cool kids. The hierarchy of the cool kids would give her a rough time and she would tell him she didn't like him because she didn't want to be embarrassed because of his status as a loser.

"I was wondering if you weren't doing anything this weekend if you would like to do something?"

"I can't," she replied.

"Can't," he repeated and watched her leave and run into the arms of her new man Mark, the jock.

"You ruined my life! You spread rumors in school that I was gay. Every woman in school believed them and it ruined me. How dare you come so far as to say you didn't mean it and that it was just a joke!" Gary exclaimed.

He twisted back his arm and lunged it forward as hard as he could into the window, breaking it. He released his anger, but felt pain in his knuckles and looked at the broken hole in the glass with blood on his right hand. He drew it back slowly while staring at the spider legs that spread across window from the hole in the glass. It reminded him that there was more to surface in his shattered life. The memories surfaced when he went to the weight room.

Gary was on the bench press, lifting ten sets of one-hundred and fifty pounds. It seemed to help get rid of his problems and move on with his future. Gary walked over to do leg squats when Mark walked in with his four jock friends.

"Get out of here, piece of shit!" yelled one of the smaller jocks.

With all the weight lifting that Gary

had done he felt confident to stick up for himself, "kiss my ass you little shit!"

Gary lied down on the bench press and began lifting the bar of weights to strengthen his arms and chest. Suddenly, he heard the sound of footsteps draw close until they got just above him. Gary got worried because he had a bar of weights over his chest and he had a feeling that they were going to screw with him.

"So I hear you said something about my mom!" said a deep voice.

Gary stopped lifting and rose up to his feet after seeing it was Mark. He could clearly see that the jock just wanted to screw with him. That's what most bullies do, prey on the innocent so they could look good and feel special.

"I never said anything about your mom and if I did I would say it to your face," said Gary.
"You want to fight?" Mark challenged as he swiftly pushed Gary against a mirrored covered wall. It shattered and pieces of it fell on the floor, which reminded Gary of his shattered life.
Mark and his imp friends grabbed Gary and held him on the bench press. Mark loaded the bar to two-hundred and fifty pounds and lifted it up with Gary's own arms and knew that Gary wouldn't be able to lift that much.
"Don't choke on it," Mark laughed and left.
Gary pushed up with all his might to

keep the bar above his neck before a couple of fellow weight lifters who walked in a few minutes later helped him so he wouldn't kill himself.

"Pieces of shattered glass, that's what seems to be left of my life!" Gary declared as he turned his head to the bath tub filled with gasoline with Mark tied up, lying in it.

"But I'm not going to let you or anyone tell me that high school life is normal. Not compared to the life I had to endure with you," said Gary as he watched Mark open his eyes and look around in terror.

"What's going on?" Mark demanded.

"I'm going to show you how you've made me feel for the course of my high school life," replied Gary as he lit his cigarette, then walked over to the bathtub and held the match up to Mark's face.

"No don't do this! I'm sorry! I was only having a little fun! I was only messing around!"

"Well, I'm sick of being messed around with and this is my way of ending it."

Gary dropped the match in the bathtub of gasoline and watched as it burst into flames. It massed around Mark's face like a swarm of bees and began burning off his flesh. Mark screamed for minutes and moved his head back in forth, quickly, like he was in a seizure. His skin began peeling off his face, revealing muscles and bone.

As the minutes persisted, Gary watched his victim's body disintegrate, leaving the smell of death in the air. He was no longer Gary August; he was the Fire Starter and now there was one less classmate that haunted him.

An Angel Visit

There was a young man named Rya, who lived a boring life. He wanted to write his novel but didn't know what he wanted it to be about. Memories unraveled in his mind as he thought about his anima during class.

She was tall with long blonde hair, thin lips, and blue eyes. Her skin was like porcelain and she was fair like a queen. He remembered her as a thirteen year old when he was upset about not being smart enough. She seemed to be more than just an imaginary friend, but someone he could confer to and feel good. Sometimes he heard her speak and she told him her name. Her name was Sarah.

The first two weeks of college life was difficult and Rya hated it. He was a rebel and noticed the students and teachers judged him because he had long hair. He argued with his physics teacher, he argued with his computer one teacher and he talked back to a student who said he could reach through his mouth and grab his pony tail. The physics teacher was surprised to see how Rya could pick up a chair in a experiment.

He wanted to find his muse in writing and didn't care for college. He was young, with light brown hair, with deep blue eyes and broad lips.

Rya woke up in the morning depressed, just as he woke up tired the day before. There was the expectations that was brought to him since he was young. He did everything to make them happy and it seemed like it was only good until it wore off. Then he would have to do something else to make them proud. It was like taking drugs so you could feel good, but drugs wear off . Rya sat in class and couldn't wait for Saturday to come.

Saturday came and after work Rya drove to Wal-mart to meet his friend Robby so they could hang out at the casino. Robby was a friend and worked at a video store for a few months.

Rya walked into Wal-mart and sat on a bench in the lay away section for Rob to meet him. A few minutes went by and a young woman walked in, looked around and sat down next to him. Rya looked at her briefly and assumed she was waiting for someone and continued to wait for his friend. After a few more minutes of being bored Rya pulled out a notebook and started writing. That's where it all started, in a notebook.

The woman was young with long black hair that was partially dyed blue halfway down the length of her hair, with black rimmed glasses. He couldn't see the color of her eyes when he looked at her briefly, but they were probably hazel.

"Excuse me, do you know what time it is?" she asked.

Rya turned his head to look at her and then his watch, "yeah, it's about six o'clock."

"Who are you waiting for?"

"My friend Rob," Rya answered.

"Is his name Rob Christensen

"I'm also waiting for Rob," she smiled and continued. "How do you know him?"

"We know each other from high school."

"My name is Krissy, Krissy Wolf, how do you do?" she introduced herself.

"Rya Finch" he answered and shook her hand.

Rya noticed something about her, something admiring, something inspiring. He looked at her eyes and could see she had brown eyes and her hair roots were brown. He was attracted to her immediately and smiled when she did.

"So what do you like to do for fun?" she asked.

"I like to write."

"You mean write books and stuff?"

"Yes," he answered.

"That's interesting, have you got anything published?" she asked

"No, not until I find my inspiration."

They talked about their goals and what they wanted to do in their life. After an hour Robby showed up and caught the end of the conversation. She was interested in foreign languages and being an interpreter.

"Hi," said Robert.

"Oh hi," they both said at once as they looked at each other and smiled.

"So what's going on?" said Rob slowly as he smiled.

"April wanted me to tell you that you forgot your CD's at her house," replied Krissy.

"Oh, I'll pick them up tomorrow," replied Rob.

"Ok" she said as she got up from the bench and turned to Rya.

"Well, it was nice to meet you," she smiled and walked away.

After she left, Rob looked at Rya with a surprise, "wow, you two sure hit it off."

"Yes we did," replied Rya with a smile.

Rob and Rya went to the Turtle Casino and met a guy who was a friend of Rob named Nick who everyone knew as Bug. They gambled for a few hours and had plenty to drink at the bar. It was Saturday night and all three were drunk and puked out their tacos. At about mid-night they took a taxi home and left their car back so they wouldn't' get nailed by the cops. When Rya hit the sack all he could think about was Krissy and how hot she was.

The next morning Rya woke up with a dry mouth. He looked at the clock to see it was one o'clock in the morning. He managed to forget most of the night but remembered from Rob that Krissy worked at Wal-mart and would be finished with her shift around four o'clock. He didn't have much time. He quickly cleaned up his room and took a shower.

He drove his car to Wal-mart and pulled into a parking spot. He knew Rob was going to call him for a ride to pick up his car at the casino. He had no idea what department Krissy worked in but started with the women's clothing area. Then there she was, dressed in her blue vest and her hair down.

"Hi," she smiled.

"Hey," he replied. "I was wondering if you would like to come back to my apartment?"

"Yeah, I get done in a half hour."

"Ok, I can wait outside the store by the bench."

"Ok," she replied as she smiled at him.

After Krissy was done with work she followed Rya home in her truck to his apartment. When they got there, they started kissing in his room. He took off her clothes and looked into her eyes just as she did the same. Her legs were nice and smooth, like her face and arms. Hours passed as they continued to touch each other while their lips remained locked and they laid in bed.

A few hours later they remained in bed and looked at each other. They didn't say anything because they were completely wiped over each other. Suddenly, they heard the outside door slam shut and footsteps echoed the house.

"Who's that?" she whispered.

"It's my Landlord. He must have come home from running his errands."

The sound of boots walked upstairs to the bedroom and minutes later they could both hear someone shooting pool. Krissy looked at the time to see it was ten thirty and gasped.

"I got to get home, I have work in the morning."
"What time you have to be there?" he asked.
"Eight o'clock."

They both got dressed and Rya walked Krissy out to her truck. She smiled at him and gave him a long passionate kiss before leaving.

He watched her back out of the driveway and smiled at her before waving good-bye. When he walked back into the house he felt like he was in love and wanted to be with her.

The week continued and everything was better. College was great because all he thought about was her. Work at the pizza job was great because she was on his mind. After school he went to visit Krissy at work and then they would make out in his room, but nothing lasts forever. He learned that she was leaving for college in Madison and wouldn't be coming back.

It was the last week of August when things became troubling. Parting ways was difficult and she became aware of it as they talked in his apartment.

"I have to go," she began. "You can't expect me to stay forever. I want to leave and make something of myself."

"What difference does it make if you make something of yourself here or anywhere else as long as we are together?"

"I want to go to college, I want to be educated and be happy."

"I'm in love with you."

Krissy looked at him in shock, "you hardly know me."

Rya was quiet for a moment before answering, "I don't need to be educated to be in love with you, but I guess I shouldn't keep you."

Krissy looked at him sternly, "don't you think that's biased?

"What do you mean, biased?"

"There's the phone, I'm not going to forget you," she replied.

"Will I hear from you?"

"Of course, as soon as I get settled in," she answered and kissed him good-bye.

Three months went by and Rya remembered watching her leave. He remembered her phone calls, but they soon stopped and he couldn't get a hold of her, she forgot about him. He fell into a depression and started failing in his classes. He stopped showing up for work and got fired.

A barrier had developed between him and the outside world. He didn't even know what time of the day it was. He didn't have any motivation to continue living and it was like the go power was completely empty.

One day, he called in sick again for his classes and stared at the wall in his room for hours. He didn't care what happened in class, he hadn't written in months. All he could think about was Krissy.

Suddenly, something strange was happening. He noticed the room turned bright white and after it ceased, stood an angel in the middle of his room. She looked very beautiful with her wings open. Rya slowly moved out of bed and drew closer to it. He could see the silhouette of her long hair extend to her knees.

Her illumination was bright, but reduced so that he could see her face. The angel looked as she did in his imagination when he was in junior high. Her blue eyes were striking and she looked at Rya as she opened her thin lips and touched her waist with her hands.

She wore a sort of white night gown that stretched to her ankles and covered her arms. The angel's wings folded behind her slender body. Her face was similar to Krissy and she spoke softly, but sternly, "if she was really your soulmate she would have come back for you."

Rya's mouth opened in shock for he didn't want to believe what he was hearing much less what he was seeing. Now this made since, he was in love with Krissy because she looked like Sarah. He thought that Sarah was his imaginary friend, but realized that she was his guardian angel.

"You know who I am," she replied calmly.

"Sarah?" he asked.

"I've been here since the beginning and have been watching over you."

"Well, then are you here in this world. I mean do you exist as a real person?" asked Rya.

Sarah spoke softly, "I'm sorry, but it doesn't work that way. Your free will has a great factor in finding your soulmate. Finding a human girl who looks like me is like looking for a specific ant out of a million and if she's not your soulmate then the work is wasted, but I can assure you all is well. Now wake up for the day and live for tomorrow. There is still plenty for you to do in this life."

"But there are so many questions I have? What is my purpose? What is it like on the other side?" Rya asked while watching her white wings spread open and the white light that had claimed the furniture drew back into her body and her face turned bright white.

"All in good time, you have much to learn and I'll be watching you. We shall meet again. All you have to do is read the signs."

Seconds later she was gone and Rya looked around in his gloomy room and began to think. An angel was here and spoke to him what a wonderful feeling. He found his muse and was healed from the depression .

His eyes opened to the sight of dawn and knew it was the beginning of a new day. He opened up his notebook and started a new story.

Krissy was gone, but his experiences and inspiration was imprinted on him forever. With a phone call to his dad he was able to get caught up on his rent and get a job at a butcher shop. It was an exhilarating moment in time and things began to turn around.

Rya continued to write and each page inspired him even more. The stagnation had broken and creativity was able to make way into his life.

When he was finished with the story he looked at the title "An Angel Visit" and put it in the envelope to be sent to the publisher. The mail man pulled into his apartment to deliver mail and Rya handed it to him. Rya looked around at the house he was looking at and the snow on the ground and realized that this was the state of his life, but soon the snow would melt and life would return again just as he had.

The Prince and the Cursed Daughter

Prince Duncan rode his horse Clovis from Castle Jaydon through the mountains and forest. He was on a mission to seek Queen Avah Epona who lived in the Kingdom of Shellmont. Prince Duncan's reddish blonde hair blew from the wind as he dodged branches that hung low from the trees. He was under competition with Prince Cometrax of Crescent Kingdom and he was uncertain as to how he would win the heart of the queen.

Slaying a dragon would do nicely if he knew where one could be found, but he was sure that something would present itself.

He was a young man that had everything given to him. He had shunned responsibility and commitment all the way, until now. He heard that Avah Epona was a seer that could see people's future and she had the power to control the weather. Duncan was egotistical and naïve as he thought to himself how he could rule over her.

It was morning and the sun was still rising overhead as it did since the beginning of time. He reached the end of the forest and came across the Magic River, which connected to the Giving Sea. The prince thought for a minute and decided to cross the river. It seemed to make more sense than riding upstream to find himself stuck with a giant lake that would keep him from crossing.

Duncan shook the reins and heard the sound of his horse let out a whinny as they rode close to the river. The sound of water hitting rocks didn't excite Clovis or motivate him to cross so the young man got off to help him walk through the water.

The water was cold and was up to his shoulders, but they persisted to cross through the river and came out of it shivering and wet.

"If you would have let me ride you I wouldn't be all wet, you stupid horse," said the prince, but all he got was a horse laughing at him through its nicker sounds, grunts and light whinnie.

Prince Duncan turned around towards the forest and saw a peculiar smoke. It seemed that there was someone close by, perhaps setting up camp.

"I see we have a lucky traveler to help me dry my clothes," said Duncan as he walked over to his horse and pulled out a folded piece of paper from his leather purse.

After unraveling it, he folded it back up and realized that they were right on course and the direction of the smoke was in direct correspondence to the Kingdom of Shellmont. The prince climbed onto his horse and shook the reins so that he could investigate the strange smoke in the forest.

Duncan traveled through ravines and hills until they reached a small clearing, just before the woods where a small cottage stood with a white picket fence. The smoke was coming from the chimney and the prince looked at his wet clothes with a smile, then at the cottage that was a long way from him.

He rode on his horse down to the house, got off and walked up to the door to knock. After knocking at the door a middle aged man answered. He was tall with hazel eyes and wore lumberjack clothes.

"What can I do for you?" asked the man.

"Pardon me sir, but I was wondering if I could seek lodging here? A place to sleep, eat and dry my clothes. My horse bucked me off in the river and I'll only be staying for a couple of days."

"Can I ask who you are?" asked the man.

"My name is Prince Duncan and I'm from the Kingdom of Jaydon."

"Oh forgive me my lord, I didn't know. Of course, you're welcome to stay as long as you like, my name is Edgemont Coleman."

Prince Duncan looked around the inside of the small cottage and stepped into a room that was the dinning and kitchen area. Duncan noticed the old man was smiling and rubbing his hands together. Then a woman entered the room. She was short with brownish grey hair and brown eyes. They were both looking at him strangely as if he was a pig waiting to be slaughtered and become the family roast.

"This is Prince Duncan and he's staying with us for a couple days" replied Edgemont.

The woman looked at Duncan while smiling and rubbed her hands together the same way he did. The prince looked at the couple disturbed, but tried to keep a straight face because he was their guest. He would only be here for the night and would be off on his journey.

"This is Mannet, my wife."
"How do you do?" asked Duncan.
"He's so handsome," she chuckled as she looked at Edgemont.
"Stenyada will be pleased with us."
"Excuse me?" asked Duncan.
"Oh Stenyada, our daughter," answered Mannet.
"Really," replied Duncan as he raised his eyebrows with a few ideas.
"She's out picking berries, but she'll be back shortly," smiled Mannet as she nodded her head.
The parent's showed him the spare bedroom that they had downstairs. It was amazing how small the house was, but it had rooms to spare. There was something confining about the whole situation. Duncan didn't really think about it, but the whole rubbing hands made him feel uncomfortable and they looked at him as though he was their last hope.

It was the act of desperation on their part that was weird. It seemed ridiculous to waste time thinking about such demands when he would be meeting Avah Epona in a few days and become king. They finally made it to his room and Edgemont pulled out the keys.

"It's the spare bedroom and I think you'll like it," replied the old man as he pushed the door open.

Inside the room there was a queen sized bed and a small table next to it with a lamp. Duncan walked inside and saw a desk and chair with pen and ink. There were also shelves of books, literature, stories and dictionaries. Cob webs covered the corners and it needed dusting, but everything else was in order. Duncan turned around and saw them smiling and rubbing their hands together.

"I'll take it," Duncan said as he pulled out a small bag of gold coins and let a few slide into his hand and handed Edgemont the money.

"Five golden coins for just helping you, your majesty?" asked Edgemont. "I couldn't. No amount of money can free me from the debt that I'm in, but if you insist I will take it," nodded the peasant.

"You can and I insist. Now if you may, I'll get settled and out of these wet clothes," said the prince.

"Oh, forgive me sire," replied the wife. "I'll be right back with some of Edgemont's clothes for you to wear until your clothes dry off," continued Mannet as she nodded and closed the door for privacy.

"Yeah, you give me some privacy or I'll lay you down on your back and give you a beating you won't forget," Duncan whispered with a smile at the dirty thought he had in mind as he took off his clothes.

After a few minutes there was a knock at the door. Prince Duncan opened the door with a towel around his waist to see it was Mannet.

"Here are some clothes until your original clothes are dried. Can I have them so that I can wash and hange them to dry?"

"Sure," replied Duncan as he handed her his wet clothes.

"Thank you, your majesty," she answered and left.

Suddenly, the prince had an idea after closing the door. He could stay awhile and satisfy his sexual appetite with their daughter. He could entice her with his experience, size and stamina. She would moan and howl all night for hours upon hours to come. Surely, she would like it like that.

Stenyada galloped on her brown horse, with a basket of black berries and saw her mother in the front washing clothes. Mannet had a big smile on her face and looked at Stenyada with excitement in her eyes. Stenyada got off her horse and walked over to her mom. Stenyada had blue eyes, black hair and was a little taller than her mother. Her broad lips plucked outward and her nose was pointy like an elf. She seemed like an ordinary girl except she was eager to get her life in gear.

"Mother is supper ready?" she asked.
"Your father is preparing it," answered Mannet. "We have company, my dear."
"Is it a man?" asked Stenyada.
"Yes and he's a prince," smiled her mom.

Stenyada cracked a grin and the wheels began to turn in her brain. It had been a long time since she had been with a man. The last man escaped and she was left to live with her parents.
"You're thirty-five years old, but you can say you're eighteen and a virgin," replied her mother with a smile. "and he will take you."

Stenyada nodded and looked at her mother as the wheels continued to turn, "I don't look that old, but I'm going to reach a point where I'll be too old to have children of my own. The last man didn't fit, the one before that couldn't satisfy me, the one before was sterile. He was good under the covers, but what's the point, if he doesn't want me?" asked Stenyada.

"Maybe this one will," answered Mannet as she raised the prince's clothes only to drop them and rubbed her hands together. The two women reached a close to their conversation and prepared for dinner.

For dinner, Stenyada wore her most attractive dress. It was an exotic blue dress and her mother decorated her hair with flowers and ribbons. Her mom also braided her daughter's hair so that she looked like a princess.

For supper they had stew, bread, butter, lamb and talked about their activities. Prince Duncan looked at Stenyada and could see how beautiful she was.

"So where are you headed?" asked Edgemont.

"I'm off to marry the queen," he answered.

"Surely the prince is keeping options open to all women," replied Mannet with a smile.

Duncan smiled while chewing his food and could sense jealousy in Stenyada's eyes. One night with their daughter would make her want him even more. He would make sure of that and she would be his slave.

"Surely the queen has many suitors to choose from," began Stenyada. "You should consider other women even if they aren't queen."

"How long until the queen makes her decision?" asked Edgemont.

"I don't know, it could be weeks, before she makes up her mind," replied Duncan.

"Father you don't mind if Prince Duncan stays longer than two days do you?" began Stenyada as she watched her father nod his head.

"Who knows maybe he'll want to stay," the girl answered as she rose up to leave and looked at him with her hypnotic wanting look. In her eyes, he could see she wanted to spend eternity with him inside her. She appeared so pleasant with her desirable figure and mature voice.

Prince Duncan watched the parents work as slaves washing dishes and putting the left-over food in the cooler, which was a compartment in the basement that was under the ground in the ice box.

The prince looked at all the family paintings and they looked as ordinary as any other family. Duncan looked around for the daughter and wondered where she had gone because he wanted to talk to her.

Edgemont and Mannet became worrisome and watched Duncan look around their home and whispered to each other so the prince couldn't hear them. The prince knew they were whispering, but didn't care because he thought they were trying to get him to marry their daughter. While the parents were busy cleaning, Stenyada walked outside in the night to look at the stars. Duncan followed her and wanted to see her.

Once outside, the prince could feel the cool wind run through his hair and heard the crickets and the birds chirp in the woods. Duncan was behind Stenyada and he watched her unravel her long black hair. It fell to her waist and she ran her fingers through it.

"I know you're here," she said.

The prince walked closer to her until he was an arm length away, "do you."

"Yes," she answered and she turned around to face him. "If I tell you something will you listen?" she asked.

"I'll listen and may even answer you," Duncan replied with a smile.

"I'm attracted to you," she slowly touched his chest with her hand and moved closer to him.

"I've waited a long time for a man such as you to come here, I've longed for it and I want you to look upon me as a princess. Will you kiss me?" Stenyada asked as her lips drew close to his.

Prince Duncan felt his heartbeat faster and faster as he felt her hands touch his diaphragm and kept going lower to his treasure trail. He closed his eyes and tried to decide what to do. His heart ruled his mind and he became desperate with her temptation. Duncan kissed and touched her face as his fingers lightly touched her neck, then her breasts.

"I want to be inside you right now," he whispered.

Stenyada and Duncan snuck back inside and ran upstairs to her bedroom. Both parents were busy with the dishes and arguing over where to move the furniture. Duncan couldn't hear the parent's bickering anymore, once he was in her room. Both became attached in a lip lock like no other and started unbuckling as well as unzipping their clothes until they were completely naked.

The hours that followed were hot and sweaty while Stenyada felt him deep inside her. She was so happy that he fit inside her and felt Duncan touch and kiss her breasts. Almost all the time he heard her say his name in the long hours.

Duncan stopped and so did Stenyada for their bodies were sore and were not use to so much lust in one night. The prince took a deep breath and lied next to her on the bed as she did the same and they slept soundly for the rest of the night. Edgemont was next to the door smiling and rubbing his hands together. He heard the prince and his daughter moaning from their sexual activity.

The next day, Stenyada and Duncan were outside next to the river laughing and talking about their dreams and drying off from skinny dipping in the river. Prince Duncan had somehow forgotten his journey to Avah Epona. After minutes of running in the rain they finally got back to the house and ran into her room for a lustful day and night of sex.

Mannet was sewing a blanket and Edgemont was reading a book looked at each other when they heard the floor boards creek and the sound of screaming upstairs.

"I'm not going to ask?" she whispered.

Edgemont put the book down and walked upstairs to Stenyada's bedroom and stood next to the door. He began smiling and rubbing his hands together as he heard his daughter orgasiming.

Stenyada jumped up and down on top of the prince lightly, moaning and yelping like a puppy, then she had another orgasm better than the last. They were both all wet and naked from the rain, but were just beginning to get hot and sweaty. Stenyada found her man and she had a feeling he would be the one to serve her day and night.

"Oh Duncan, will you be mine forever?" she asked while embracing him tightly.
"Yes," he said.

With the last thrust that shook the bed they both stopped to breathe and as they lied down together as she kissed him. Duncan felt her loving lips touch his neck and they tickled his insides with laughter. He thought to himself *why pursue the queen of Shellmont when he had the woman of his dreams right in front of him?* Edgemont continued to smile from behind the door and rubbed his hands together.

A few weeks went by and the prince helped the family with the chores, but today would be different and they were joined by Stenyada. She sat at the table and looked at her father who was smiling. The prince acted like nothing was out of the ordinary as they were about to eat breakfast.

"I'm pregnant," said Stenyada.

Mannet looked at her daughter in surprise and Edgemont clapped his hands together. The prince's eyes opened wide in shock since he didn't expect this to happen. Stenyada began to smile at the prince, a smile that said without words *I have you now, my prince.*

"Well, I'm going to be packing," laughed Edgemont as he got up.

"I don't understand," replied the prince.

"You freed us from the curse of living with her."

"Hey, you're not leaving!" exclaimed Stenyada.

"I have the power to keep you here."

Edgemont started laughing "the only reason you have power over me is because I slept with your mother to get my fill and she took away all my dreams you little whore!"

Stenyada started to cry and looked at her mother, "mother you aren't leaving me are you?"

"I'm sorry daughter, but I am. You were such a blessing, but as soon as you turned twelve you became a nightmare," replied her mother as Stenyada watched everyone leave the table.

"What are you doing with my horse?" asked the prince as he saw Edgemont packing everything on his horse.

"I'm stealing it," began Edgemont.

"Say good-bye to your life. Stenyada's your wife and you won't be able to do anything. Here's a little advice, kill yourself now and don't wait like I did."

"So, I was nothing more than a pawn?" asked Duncan.

"Yes," answered Edgemont. "Thankyou for being the dumb jackass!"

Prince Duncan stared at the old man who he thought was nice and pleasant as his mouth dropped, "what about Mannet?"

Edgemont shook his head and the reins to escape, "the bitch can be swallowed up by the ground for all I care."

The prince turned around to see Mannet was dressed in a cloak with a bag of possessions and was leaving as well. Stenyada was behind her and looked upset. Prince Duncan watched her leave the cottage and she waved good-bye to Stenyada.

Minutes went by and Duncan walked back into the cottage, packed up his things and was about to leave. He acted like his usual self and ignored what had happened. He was a prince that paid no mind to responsibilities and a man that didn't care about the women he caused broken hearts to.

"Where do you think you're going?" demanded Stenyada in a cold tone, who had a feeling he would leave her with his child.

"I'm leaving to marry the queen of Shellmont," replied Duncan as he watched her mouth drop. "Don't fret, you knew this was going to happen. You knew that our nights together would be empty, but full of lust and that's all you are is a whore," continued the prince as he turned to leave.

"You're not going anywhere!" she exclaimed in a loud scream. "You think I would give you my heart, soul and a beautiful child only to have you abandon me?"

The prince turned around and hesitated before speaking, "yes I do, just as your father said you're a whore, I am of royal blood and I'm going to marry the queen."

"No, you're not a prince! You belong to me," demanded the cursed daughter. "Your new purpose is to serve me everyday for the rest of your life and you will love me as well as our daughter!" shouted Stenyada.

Suddenly, Duncan felt a piercing sensation in his heart and fell to the ground. Stenyada was using her power to bring the prince to his knees which was telekinetic. The prince felt excruciating pain in his rectum as well as his stomach and began crying. Stenyada began to grimace as a sneer emerged on her face that she was hiding something special all along which was her abilities.

"I've got special powers to get what I want and you will submit to me," she ordered.

The prince began screaming in horror as he tried to run for the door with each stumbling step and held his diaphragm. He felt like he was exploding and made it as far as the picket fence.

Suddenly, something grabbed and pulled him back to the open door where the cursed daughter was standing, watching him stumble to get away. He flew through the air backwards and into the house before the door slammed shut.

The crows and ravens heard the prince screaming and squawked as they raised their wings. They flew away and in the distance the screams became harder to hear and the house became silent beyond the trees so no one would bother the prince and the cursed daughter.

The Black Widows

Glenada had traveled on his horse, Atrax, for three days into an unexplored territory. He was mapping a route to find an alternative way to travel to the towns on the other side of the contenent to find work, instead of traveling through the mountains.

Glenada was a gladiator and he was thirsty so he picked up his canteen of water and took a sip. The young man with green eyes, black hair and bristly face could see that Atrax was getting spooked from the trees. The twenty-year old gladiator could feel the heat from the sun and felt sweat drip from his forehead. He was wearing a black tunic with a black colored armor covering his chest. His muscular arms could be revealed and he wore a black cape that extended to his knees, just over his tunic. There was no river or lake in the area and he hoped that there would be some sort of settlement where he could lodge to continue mapping his rout.

The forest was thick and the trees were close together; a lot of them were intertwined into each other. He continued on foot and found a big house made of stone and brick. It was the size of a mansion with a strange roof made of leaves and branches.

"Who do you suppose lives here?" he whispered to his horse.

Glenada tied his horse to a nearby tree branch and walked to the front door. There was a gold bell with a sign inscribed; *guests ring bell.*

A few minutes went by and after ringing the bell a girl that looked about six years old answered. She had black hair tied in braided pigtails with grey eyes and wore a strange black dress.

"Is your mother home?" he asked.
"Yes," she answered with a straight face that turned into a creepy smile.
Then an older girl with long black hair and grey eyes walked up to the door, "hello, my name is Cora and this is my little sister Tara."
"My name is Glenada and I'm exploring this region. I'm from the town of Oxford."

Cora was quiet because she was looking at his mighty arms and then she turned to look at the gladiator's tan face. He looked at her strangely and wondered why she was feasting her eyes over him like a piece of meat. She nodded her head and smiled at the gladiator, which gave him chills.

"Yes," she began. "You must join us for supper, my mother is downstairs teaching my sister Malaria how to mend an incision.
"It wouldn't be for long, I would be gone the next morning," he answered
"Oh, but I'm sure you would want to stay longer than that, come in," she insisted with a smile.
Glenada walked in to their home and straight ahead of him was fancy furniture made of wood with sewn pillows created with complex designs of black widows. He saw a fireplace and on the edge of the fireplace were life size human statues, one a man and the other a woman, made of wood. They were both naked and holding up a stone ledge above the fireplace that was full of stone and crystal knick knacks.

"I'll fetch our mother," Cora replied and left Tara to watch Glenada.

Scarlet was in the cellar with her daughter Malaria and they were sewing up a long cut on a man's abdomen. She was teaching her daughter the value of patience. As an apprentice, Malaria was learning the craft of an amazonian that was passed by Scarlet.

"Dear, you want the stitches small and tight so they can't get out," said Scarlet while showing Malaria each piercing stitch of the needle through the skin.

"Like that?" asked Malaria.

"Yes," answered Scarlet as she clasped her hands together.

"Once you get done, you want to put this ointment on the wound and spread it around so it gets nice and hard. Remember it acts as a sealant so that we can continue to pounce on him everynight. This will increase our chances of expanding our community and his body heat will allow them to hatch. Once he's been eaten from the inside your sister will brush the rest of the ointment on his body. After he's been hardened, we can make him into a statue and place him somewhere in the yard for decoration," announced Scarlet as she turned to see Cora staring at her.

"Oh hi dear, what news do you bring?"

"We have a traveler here."

"Oh, is he healthy?"

Cora raised her shoulders, "I don't know."

Scarlet looked at Malaria and gestured her to continue the work, "well, I guess we'll have to see what kind of man we have."

Glenada walked around the living room which was painted white with black spider webs and Tara watched him quietly with a creepy stare. The gladiator could see the wooden floor was swept and the furniture was white with gold tassels for trimming on the bottom.

On the wall next to the staircase was a wooden desk which held a shelving unit filled with silver figurines of men, dragons and flying horses. The site of crystals around the knick knacks caught his attention, but it shifted as he looked at the fireplace and walked over to it. He could see a giant Venus Fly Trap on top of the ledge with the two wooden statues. As he looked closer at the statue of the muscular man and woman he could see they were in pain.

"Well hello stranger," said a voice.

Glenada turned around to see it was a woman and guessed it was the mother. She was dressed in a plain brown dress and her black hair was tied back into a pony tail. The woman was strange, with the tone in her voice that was deep and scratchy. Her grey eyes feasted upon him like a vampire and she licked her lips while looking at his muscular arms. Scarlet thought to herself that this man would have enough endurance to keep her satisfied.

"You've got quite a place here, who built your house?" he asked while walking towards her.
"Men," she replied with the tone in her voice that was cold and dis-satisfied.
"My name is Glenada; I'm exploring this region and discovered your home. I was wondering if I could stay here for the night?"
"My name is Scarlet and you may stay for as long as you like," replied Scarlet as Malaria came up to see him.

Glenada was directed to a room upstairs and the three daughters followed from behind. He was told that they were virgins and hadn't seen a good looking guy for quite a long time. Scarlet opened the door and let him in as she looked at his buttocks and then his arms.

She began to smile as he turned around, "it's a plain room, but I hope it will do for the night."

Glenada smiled back and nodded, "it will do."

Scarlet nodded and closed the door. After the door closed, the gladiator looked around the old room with cobwebs in the corner and thought the mom and her daughters were creepy.

The women grouped together to prepare supper and Glenada could smell the rich aroma of food from his room. There was a knock at the door and Glenada answered to see it was Tara.

She smiled at him, "would you like to eat supper with us?"

"Yes," he answered.

Glenada ate plentiful with the group of women and they enjoyed his company. Scarlet looked at him and winked to see if he was interested in her, but all he did was smile. They talked about their history together and the house as the gladiator talked about where he was from. It got late and they retired; the warrior went to sleep early that night to get an early start tomorrow.

Then one night the gladiator opened his eyes after hearing loud moaning and screaming. He got dressed and got all his possessions in gear before he left his room to follow the moaning. It was dark and he lit a candle that he had in his bag. He walked downstairs; came across a door and peeked through the crack of the door to see what was going on.

He saw Scarlet was on top of a man, having sex and screaming. The man she was on top of was pale and looked like he was in a lot of pain. Cora and Malaria were watching as he moved his head back and forth, screaming while something began crawling out of his mouth. They were black widow spiders, the size of silver dollars and they began walking quickly over his sweaty chest and onto Scarlet's breasts. She raised her arms up to the ceiling to an even bigger spider that was up in the ceiling.

"I give you this sacrifice Great Vega sister to the Succubus and give you the birth of your children. All I ask of you is to protect our home and expand our community."

The man was dead when she got off of him and let the black widows jump from her to the ground. Glenada suddenly realized what they had planned for him.

"That's how it's done," she began. "Their purpose is to enable us to expand our numbers. They're not meant to be our masters or our equals, but to be our dogs."

"We have the ability to create babies that can become men," replied Cora.

"Why is it wrong to have them?" asked Malaria.

"Because my daughters they grow up to be men and they'll try to rule us and so you must kill them. Now we can wheel the other two beds around and you try."

Cora and Malaria nodded as they removed their clothes and looked excited to participate in the ritual. They continued where their mother left off and began pouncing and thrusting their pelvis on the helpless two men that were chained. They swung back and forth then quickly again as they began to feel enjoyment. After hours of pouncing, the girls watched things move under the men's skin. They paid no mind and were busy satisfying themselves as both men turned pale.

"Stop, please, I feel like I'm being eaten alive from the inside out," screamed the man that was being pounced on by Cora.

"Don't worry! I'll take perfect care of you when I turn you into a statue," sneered Cora as the sweat rolled off her forehead and onto the man's face.

A few minutes went by and the black widows started coming out of the two men who were going through convulsions. The baby spiders emerged from the men's mouths and swarmed around both girls' sweaty bodies to bond with them.

Scarlet was overjoyed and relieved that now both girls were accepted in the job of birthing the black widows. She would no longer have to worry about enlarging the community herself, now that her daughters were capable.

Cora and Malaria got off the guys and pet the baby spiders and listened to them purr like baby kittens. The baby spiders jumped off the girl's bodies and scattered to the walls and ceilings to get to the big spider above.

Glenada had seen enough and turned around to leave when he came face to face with Tara. She stared at him with her eerie grey eyes and was quiet as she watched him become scared. Her mother told her that if any man was caught snooping by the door to let her know.

Tara let out a dreaded scream that was loud enough to wake the dead. The gladiator didn't have the heart to slay her so he left the house.

Scarlet, Malaria and Cora came outside the forbidden door in their robes to see the screaming child. Tara calmed down as Cora and Malaria held her.

"The man was watching through the door!" cried Tara.

"Damn," exclaimed Scarlet.

"And I wanted to use your teachings on him mother," replied Malaria as they followed Scarlet to the entrance of the door only to find the gladiator gone.

Glenada was on his horse charging through the woods like there was no tomorrow. They journeyed for the next couple of miles nonstop until he realized that the Black Widow Amazonians weren't pursuing him and stopped to rest.

"I'll never make a pit stop to a house like that again!" exclaimed the gladiator and Atrax let out a whinny in agreement.

The Insect Behind My Eye

The lost boy gripped the handle bars of his bike. His objective was to get home and he could feel an adrenaline rush throughout his body. His eyes were shiny and with a smile, he pumped his legs up and down to generate speed on his mountain bike.

It was three in the morning that he left work and as he turned off the highway he thought how wonderful it was now that he wouldn't have to stare at the bright headlights of incoming cars. It would be country roads all the way to his house. He shook the anxiety of being hit by a car and biked faster down the country road. He thought of himself as the Midnight Biker because he biked at night and it made him feel like a gunslinger.

He felt the wind hit his face and wiped the sweat from his cheeks. Suddenly, something flew in his ear and he lost control. The kid fell off his bike and collapsed onto the pavement. He looked around, realizing he was in the middle of the road and felt pain in his knee as well as something moving in his ear canal. He could hear chewing and the fluttering that sounded like wings. It was trying to move even further down his ear canal and it hurt.

There was a light at the end of the dark tunnel for the gunslinger. He walked to a well-lit house that was about a hundred feet away, across the street. The fluttering and chewing continued and he thought it was going to reach his brain.

The biker knocked at the door, but nobody answered. He became impatient and scared as he knocked again, but harder.

"Come on," he cried.

Suddenly, he saw the door bell, and hit it. He waited until two people came to the door and they looked at him apprehensively. One was a man wearing his pajamas and held a handgun. His wife was behind him in her nightgown and they huddled behind the door.

"Can we help you?" asked the man.

The Midnight Biker cried, "there's something in my ear and I want to know if you can see it?"

He could see the man was determined not just to protect his house and wife, but also to kill anyone who bothered him late at night to look in someone's ear.

"I don't see anything," answered the man.

"I'm not putting on a show, and have no interest in robbing you. I have something in my ear!"

Slowly the man came out from his door to get a better look at the biker. He looked confused at him and thought he was insane. He cocked his gun as though he was expecting anything.

"No I don't see anything," he answered.

The gunslinger felt anguish because there was no way to show what was in his ear. He wished he had some way to prove it, but even he didn't know what was in his ear. It probably was a small bat and it was trying to squeeze into his ear to create a nest. That's all the lost boy needed, a bat making a home in his brain.

"Where do you live?" asked the man.
The young man cried in pain as he pointed to the road, "I just live up the road from here!"

The pain and fluttering of the insect living in his ear hurt. The lost boy could not determine what it was like to experience the pain with any other specific feeling. He gathered what strength he had to get home.

"Will you be all right?" asked the man.
The lost boy let out a sigh as he touched his right ear with agony and lied, "I'll be fine."

As he left, he knew he made himself look like an ass by going to a stranger's house complaining that something was in his ear when they couldn't see what was in his ear in the first place.
He could not bike the same as he did before the incident. He was unbalanced for what seemed like an eternity of madness.

When he got home, he cried, "mother, mother, I have something in my ear!"

His mother woke up to see what her son was screaming about. It was five in the morning and she was half asleep. Her warm tenderness calmed him down and tried to figure out what was wrong.
"I don't see anything, try using the water in the faucet or Q-Tips," she suggested.

After sticking his ear to the faucet failed and the Q-tips caused more harm than good he began to get restless.

"It's not working!" he screamed.

His mother had just gotten off the phone with the doctor who told her to use a water dropper. His mother stuck the muzzle of the filled water dropper in his ear. The pure triumph to get it out was a top priority for her son. She tried to get the bothersome pain from his ear, but failed. His mother called the doctor again.

"Doctor, it didn't work, the thing is still in his ear," said his mother and there was a brief silence for a moment. "Ok, I'll bring him tomorrow," continued his mother.

The lost boy withered in pain as the fluttering and chewing got worse. It hurt even more as he laid on his ear. He ached in pain and felt the creature move even deeper, driving him mad.

"I made an appointment for you in the morning with the doctor. All I can say is sleep on it for now," said his mother.

"Sleep on it! Are you for real? How am I supposed to sleep with this thing in my ear?" asked the lost boy.

His mother handed him a heating pad that had been used to treat ear aches. In agony, the Mid-night Biker tried to get to sleep and brought the heating pad to its maximum temperature. Before he knew it he was asleep but had nightmares of a creature eating his brain and laying its eggs inside of him. He couldn't get any sleep with the nightmares of the insect behind his eye.

The next morning the biker and his mother went to the doctor. He was hoping the doctor had a better way

of getting whatever it was out of his ear. He looked
around at all the people that were waiting for the doctor
with their own problems. Immediately when they sat
down; they were directed by a nurse to undergo a series
of tests and procedures. He cried in pain from his ear
and felt like he was going to lose his ear in an
amputation procedure.

"We believe there is a baby bat inside your ear,"
replied the nurse. The young man was frantic and didn't
know what to think. The hysteria of him ever being
normal again or the same, was now forgotten.

How could he ever return home or school for
that matter? The gunslinger could just see it now and
hear the baby bat crying; "mommy, mommy, milk, milk,
I want to get out!"

The doctor entered the room and did a number
of tests and asked questions for the young man. He was
getting agitated because the doctors were all the same.
The doctor didn't know what kind of pain he was in but
it was only escalating the problem.

"There is definitely something in your ear,
"answered the doctor.

"You think? I don't care what it is, all I know is
that it's in my ear and its got to go!" exclaimed the lost
boy as the doctor gave him a smile.

The doctor nodded understanding the young
man's pain. He went to get a physician's water dropper
that was huge, a king sized one. To end the pain and
misery of his patient he would have to get in deep in the
ear canal. The Mid-night Biker felt the fluttering and
chewing persist. He knew he didn't want to spend the
rest of his life like this.

"Do it, "demanded the lost boy.

The doctor applied the water dropper into his ear and with a slight pain of the water pressure he felt no more fluttering or chewing. Whatever it was that slumbered in his ear was now dead and floating in a small dish.

"We got it," declared the doctor. The young man looked to see it with his own eyes and couldn't believe it.

"Well, I'll be dammed it's a water bug!"

She Says

Barber placed his hand in his grandmother's cold, clammy, hand. His grandma was sleeping in her bed, at the group home, just as she had for the past ten years. His stomach filled with butterflies not knowing where to begin. Her subtle breathing and closed eyes revealed she was in another world. Barber pretended she was awake and listening as he leaned closer to her.

"Hi grandma, how are you doing today?"

There was no answer; her condition hadn't changed for the past four months and the phone call from the nursing home urged him to see her today. Barber looked outside to see the snow blowing in the wind. It was cold outside, more than any other day but it was the intuition that grandma was leaving that he dreaded most. He rested his head on her warm chest and could hear her heartbeat. Then slowly, he lifted his head as he wiped his eyes and looked at her.

"I'm so happy to see you today," he said as the tears rose from his eyes.

"There is so much I want to say to you and I don't know where to begin," he choked in a laugh and wiped his eyes again.

"My mom, dad and sister got to visit Paris with my sister as a field trip the school set up. She's having the time of her life, but she's thinking of you. Caroline finished her floral design and has a certificate. May is almost finished with ninth grade and will be a sophomore," he said as he took a minute. He thought about when he was young and was at the house watching tv with her.

"You're special to me grandma and I want you to know that. You were always there for us," his voice trembled as he revealed a smile on his face to re-live the memories in his life.

One of the memories gave him pleasure to re-live and made him laugh. It filled his soul like a picture of water pouring into a flower bed filled with roses. It was this memory that unfolded in such flashbacks.

>"Grandma can we play checkers?" asked Barber as he lifted the checkerboard for her to see. Beneath the thick glasses his grandma grinned at the young eight year old.
>
>"Set it up!" she smiled.
>
>Barber placed the pieces on the board until she was finished cooking the soup on the stove. He was black, she was red and when it was all set up he made the first move.
>
>"Hey Grandma, what is that big wooden thing on the book shelf?"
>
>"It's a nut," she answered and carefully moved her round checker.
>
>"The stuff in the dark wooden dresser down stairs, who's is it?" he asked as he moved his checker piece.

*"That belonged to your grandpa;
someday when you're older you can have it,"
she answered before moving her red checker
piece.*

*Barber quickly double jumped two
checker pieces. His grandma hesitated for a
minute realizing what had happened.*

*"I think you're cheating," she
chuckled.*

*After the game, they spent the hour
reading Three Little Pigs and The Gingerbread
Man. They ate chicken sandwiches and
vegetable soup while they talked about the
importance of saving money. Save your pennies,
dimes and nickels is what she would always say.*

*"In school I can run like the
Gingerbread Man," Barber insisted as his
grandma laughed. The powerful taste of ginger
snaps and Fig Newton's filled his stomach with
such delight.*

*He didn't want it to end and when he
was that young, time stood still. Surely grandma
could live forever to play checkers and read
Three Little Pigs.*

"We had a lot of good times, grandma. Every
year on Thanksgiving and Christmas we would play
Monopoly. Every summer I would mow your lawn
and you would pay me twenty dollars for doing it. I
remember you telling me the value of saving money to
accomplish your dreams. I think back on it and would
give every cent of it back just so you could rejoice with
me right this second the way you did when I was
young," said Barber as he lightly caressed his hand over

her forehead and into her grey, curly hair.

He sat in her bed and looked at her as he tried to think about all the things she said. Barber could still hear grandma's voice inside his head and when she visited him at school in second grade for grandparent's day he felt special. She nurtured him when he was sick and he helped her get out of bed when he was older. Grandmas and grandpas are very important to the world, but his grandma was his second mom.

"You know what the happiest day of my life is?" Barber whispered into her ear. "The day I graduated from high school; I was getting ready that morning for the ceremony and you called my house. I could tell you were crying on the other end of the phone and you were so happy for me, you wished you could be there to watch me walk.

I was in tears on the phone when you congratulated and told me how you felt. Caroline told me how surprised you were when she showed you her prom dress. Caroline told me you thought she was an angel. All the times when Lanet and I would get into fights and you would break us apart. Well, we settled our differences and get along better than we ever have before. There is one thing that you were right about with May, my baby sister. When she was five years old you knew she would be smart and an honor roll student. Well grandma you were right, she is smart! She is so smart that I tell her to not put herself down when she is faced with a problem that I know I never could've broken down at her age."

It was the morning before the field trip to Paris and Barber's mom was sitting at the kitchen table with the family. Barber walked upstairs to take a shower and wish them luck on their trip.

"Barber come here," his mother insisted and the two met at the table.
"I had a dream that grandma's going to pass away while we're gone. Can you and Caroline visit her while we're gone?"
"Yes, of course," Barber said because he knew there wasn't much time. He knew the dream was prophetic right from the start. After his parent's departure and talking to his sisters he made it a high priority to visit.

"Grandma there is so much I wish that we could do together. I wish I was seven years old again to relive those moments of picking blackberries in the hot summer to drinking hot chocolate in the cold blizzards while playing Old Maid. My mom told me something that you once told her, when I was teasing the kids at school. If you haven't got anything nice to say, then don't say anything. That is something that I, to this day, keep in mind whenever someone makes me mad."

Barber looked at his clock to see it was three-thirty in the afternoon and was unhappy that it was time to go to work. He dried his eyes with a kleenex and bent his head over and gave his grandma a kiss good-bye.

"I love you grandma, I got to go, but I'll be back soon," he assured her and left.

The terrible anxiety began in the middle of Barber's shift while unloading the second trailer at One Way Ship Service. He could hear his grandma's voice and remembered her talking about dying during past visits, but she fought hard to be with the family. It was hurting him, it was driving him crazy and he got the impression that the last hours were at hand.

He stepped out of trailer, took a deep breath and walked to his supervisor, "I got to go, now!"

"What is the problem?" he asked.

"My grandmother needs me, I think she's about to pass away. I can't concentrate on my job!" demanded Barber.

"OK, go see her," replied the supervisor and Barber left.

Barber could feel his heart pound as he ran to the parking lot. He dug into his pockets for the keys and found them. He turned the car on and peeled out of the parking lot as quickly as possible.

He arrived at the group home, locked the doors and ran inside. The brief smell of the nursing home and warm air gave him a foreboding feeling. He looked along the walls for grandma's name and found her room. He peered inside the room to find a young nurse changing the bed spread, the bed was empty.

Barber began to choke as his throat felt dry. He was thinking and hoping she was maybe switched to another room.

"Where's my grandma?"

The nurse looked at him with sadness, but before she spoke he backed away. Barber began to shake his head, not wanting to believe it and not wanting to accept it.

"No," he cried, but in his mind he was screaming it.

He left and sat in his car and started crying. If only he took off work to stay with her, if only he stayed with her, if only he talked to her more and motivated her to stay alive then none of this would have happened. How stupid he was for leaving and why did he leave? He left to go to work. Why didn't he just call in and stay? He felt guilty for not choosing the last few minutes with grandma, maybe she would have held on. Why? Why? Why? The question repeated, haunting him and his stomach hurt as he saw a replay of his life with grandma from the beginning of his life to the end of hers.

"Grandma," he cried.

Then he realized she gave him more than he had known and it was wisdom that made him who he was today. What was he to tell his sister and most of all his mother who had the dream that grandma was going to pass away while she wasn't around. He could still see her face and hear her laughter. After he settled down he decided to go home.

With the slow turn of the key he heard the ignition of his car start up and headed home. The car pulled up the driveway and looked at the door of the house, he didn't know what he was going to say to Caroline. He approached the door of his house and felt hesitant to break the news to his sister, but he knew hea had to.

He turned the door knob and walked inside to feel the house shake when he slammed the door. Only the illuminating light from a lamp upstairs filled the living room, but there was no happiness only a sad soft illumination of emptiness in the atmosphere. Barber walked upstairs to see his sister sitting cross-legged on the sofa. He didn't have to speak for he saw in her eyes that she already knew. He took off his jacket and set it on the rail.

"Grandma's gone," sobbed Caroline.

"I know," Barber answered and slowly walked up to the couch to sit down.

"She was in so much pain, I told her that if she wanted to go, that it was ok for her to go," continued Caroline as she cried.

"What time did you see her?" he asked.

"I saw her this evening at four o'clock," replied Caroline as she tried to stop crying, but couldn't.

Barber looked into his sister's eyes and felt a weight had been lifted. Grandma wasn't alone and Caroline arrived after he left. He saw her lips tremble as she all of a sudden hugged Barger and began balling. It was through her eyes that Barber could see that grandma met just as much to her as she did to him.

"Grandma was crying! I could see she was crying," sobbed Caroline.

"I stayed as long as I could and then I just had to leave because it was too painful to be there. I got the call from the nursing home after I got home and I couldn't believe it. I didn't want to believe it!" She broke into tears again as Barber hugged his sister while feeling the pain

"Sshh its ok, she will always be with us," replied Barber as he remembered Grandma's smile when he and his sister were children.

The Gay Fairies

"Hey, you can't sit here!" exclaimed Mark as he stared at Ray. "Go sit with the queers."

Ray sat by himself at a table from everybody. He hated junior high because the students always treated him like a piece of trash. Ray dreamed of the day he would become one of the cool people. He was never good enough to play sports and there were untrue rumors that spread about his sexuality.

The young man looked around the cafeteria and could see how disgusting most of the popular kids were. He couldn't understand why pretty, popular, girls would go out with ugly cool guys because he wanted to go out with them.

The buzzer rang and he went to his social studies class with Mr. Lewis. As soon as Ray sat in his desk he could hear the same popular kids talking about him.

"Hey Ray, do you spend all night dreaming about playing swords with other guys or do you play butt darts?" laughed Billy.

"No, he goes around and has sex with skunks," laughed Mark.

"I heard he likes gerbils," giggled Danny.

"No, he spends his nights dreaming about it."

"I'm not gay," answered Ray.

"Yeah right," replied Mark.

Jason started laughing, "gerbils like up there."

A jock started acting like a gerbil by moving his hands in and out like he was moving a curtain to a movie theater.

The day came to an end and Ray got on the bus only to see the same kids were on the bus. Right away, Ray sat in the front seat to avoid being teased and kept to himself with his homework. Suddenly, something hard hit him in the back of the head. It was an apple core and Ray began to get upset, but not as mad as he got when he heard some of the same jocks chant together; *Ray is gay, Ray is gay, Ray is gay*

He hated being on the bus and school. Ray wasn't learning anything interesting and was constantly dis-respected. It was obvious that he wasn't welcomed in his grade and would never be accepted.

Ray left the bus and walked to his house. He opened the door and walked inside. His mother Adias was making supper and the television was on a re-run of, The Peoples Court.

"Hey honey, how was your day?" she asked.
"I hate school!" yelled Ray as he ran upstairs.
"That's nice dear," said his mother as she continued cooking.

Ray went to bed that night and hoped that he would find peace in his dreams. He slipped under the covers after turning off the lights and snuggled in his warm bed.

The next morning Ray woke up and walked to the bathroom to get ready for school. There was something strange going on because the sun was shining through the windows and he knew it was November. Every day during this time of year was dark by the time four o' clock rolled around the corner. Ray scratched his head and jumped in the shower to wash away the nightmare of yesterday. Unexpectedly he heard the whispers of girls in the bathroom.

"Is he in there?"
"I think so," answered a voice.

Ray opened the shower curtain to find five girls wearing hardly any clothes with dragonfly wings looking at him. They smiled with love in their eyes and looked like they were pieces of candy because they were so glittery.

Ray rubbed his eyes to look again at them and couldn't believe he was being visited by fairies.

"Are you gay?" asked the first, who had whitish blonde hair. The other fairies had red, black, brown and yellowish blond hair and they looked at him curiously. They were dressed in leaves across their breasts and private areas.
"What the hell is this? Can't you see I'm taking a shower to get ready for school?"
"We're looking for jolly-good-lucky, shiny, gay people," said the burnet.   "Well, go find them and leave me alone!" said Ray as he closed the shower curtain.
"Come on, let's go, he's not gay."
"But Aura, I heard he was gay, can't we stay?"
"No, we can only stay if he's gay," said the other.
"Can we make him gay? He looks kind of sad, maybe we can cheer him up."

Without another word they disappeared and Ray continued his shower.
When he was finished, he stepped out of the shower and walked to his room with a towel tied around his waist. He was looking in the mirror and washing his face when the whitish blonde hair fairy emerged from out of the mirror.

"Are you gay?"

Ray screamed and stumbled backwards onto the bed where the four other fairies were. They touched his shoulders and were smiling at him, which made him uneasy. Ray's eyes opened wide as he tried to stay calm.

"Hi Ray," they said together smiling.

"What do you want?" he asked.

"Nothing," said the brown haired one.

"What are you?" he asked.

"We're fairies and we've been sent by Ayana of the King's Daughters to enter this world of the forbidden and bring love to those who deserve it," said the red head fairy.

Ray took a deep breath and looked from one fairy to the next with a sigh. The whitish blonde hair fairy flew out of the mirror and fluttered around him with her wings moving quickly like a humming bird.

"My name is Aura," said the whitish blonde hair fairy.

"My name is Aurora," said the golden blonde hair fairy.

"My name is Tea," said the brown haired fairy.

"My name is Tenaya," said the red haired fairy.

"My name is Lavender," said the black haired fairy.

"And we are the Gay Fairies," they said together.

Ray rolled his eyes and took a deep breath before thinking to himself; what did I do to deserve this? He looked at the little fairies that were the size of little twelve year old girls. They were very exotic and cute with the sparkles that covered their bodies.

"So you make humans into gays?" he asked.

"We try to make humans into shiny, sparkly, gay people," said Aurora.

"Humans have the tendency to become dependent on other people making them gay," added Aura.

"Being gay is the best thing for humans to be," said Tea.

"Why is that?" asked Ray.

"Well, think about it? If all humans could be gay then there would be no wars or hatred towards one another," continued Tea.

"Humans would be busy spawning to produce more gay humans," added Lavender.

"So you're here to make me gay?" asked Ray.

"Precisely" answered Tenaya.

"We'll shine you up and make you sparkly," added Aura.

"No!" shouted Ray.

"Don't you want to be gay?"

"No I don't want you to shine me up or sparkle me into a homo!"

"Homo?" repeated Aura. What is that?"

All the fairies huddled together like a football team and began talking among themselves. Ray began to groan and whine as he wondered what he did to provoke God to be harassed by these little demons. Ray continued to listen to the fairies talk and almost laughed at what he was hearing.

"I don't know what a homo is?" said one of them.

"I think it's when a guy likes a donkey" said another.

"*I think we can make him gay,*" replied another.

"*Let's just come back tomorrow and help him.*"

Ray rolled his eyes and realized that this torment wasn't going to end so he had to make a decision. When it rains lemons then you make lemon-aid and when someone wants to make your life miserable do the exact opposite of what they expect.

"*Fairies fairies, fairies,*" he repeated.

The Gay Fairies turned around and looked at him. Aura and Aurora began to smile as Lavender giggled. They thought how cute he was and how gay he would be when they got done with him.

"*I'll tell you what; I'll let you make me gay if you do me a favor.*"

"*What's that?*" they asked together.

"*You come to my school and make the humans gay that harass me and spread rumors about me being gay,*" he said

"*Let's get started,*" began Tenaya.

"*Yeah, we want to make you gay before the sun goes down,*" laughed Aura.

The fairies spent hours in the bath tub putting on sparkly solutions in his hair and face and then massaging his shoulders. He spent hours in the bathtub getting a back massage from Aura and getting his feet massaged by Lavender. He could hear them singing in rhymes that were in a fairy language.

The other fairies were busy putting ointment on his face. The young man could see huge bubbles in the bathroom and the sunlight that went through the window caused rainbows to shine on the walls.

Ray got out of the bathtub and looked in the mirror to see his skin was clear. He looked even more attractive and when he smiled it almost scared him to look this good.

"You see, you look so gay," replied Aura.

Ray shook his head, "I thought you were going to make me fall in love with guys. If I would have known you were going to do this I would have said yes."

"Fall in love with guys?" asked Aura as she turned to repeat what Ray just said to the other fairies.

Lavender started laughing, "oh, those kind."

"We don't do that," replied Tenaya.

"We follow the laws of freewill governed by Ayana to help make all humans gay," replied Aurora.

Ray stopped looking in the mirror and turned around to look at all five fairies. He looked surprised and began to realize that they were a blessing to have around. They all continued to smile at him and then he smiled back.

"He looks so gay," repeated Tenaya.

Ray woke up and realized it was all a dream. He got up and walked to the bathroom and looked at himself. He looked the same and wondered what the point of the dream was. The young man checked the time to see it was ten minutes to seven in the morning and he was falling behind schedule. He quickly ate breakfast and ran out to catch the bus.

The day seemed normal for Ray until lunch time when he got his food and was preparing to sit at the table full of jocks. He felt a knot in his stomach and hoped that today would be different than yesterday. It wasn't, and he felt the leader of the jocks test him again.

Mark gave him a dirty look, "hey homo didn't I tell you to go sit with the queers!"

"Well I would, but you see they want you to sit with them," answered Ray.

Then the kids started chanting his name to get him upset. Instead of leaving the table Ray ignored them and kept eating.

"Ray you're such a homo, why don't you go screw a cow!" yelled Mark.

"Ok," answered Ray as he kept eating.

Suddenly, Mark and his friends left the table to sit somewhere else. Ray was all alone to eat and it was just as well. He was better off without them and knew it was the beginning of something better.

Then a wonderful thing happened; all the beautiful girls in his grade sat at his table and greeted him, "Hey Ray, how are you?"

They said one after the other, "how is your day?"

Ray looked around and couldn't believe that all these gorgeous young ladies switched tables to sit with him. They were talking and laughing about things that he could only dream about. The rest of the day went well and the Gay Fairies watched from a distance outside a window above the tables, looking in and laughed together.

"He's so gay," said Aura.

Willy And Alley's Greatest Adventure

Willy woke up excited and wondered what the day would bring. He was a white colored cat just like his mom with one eye blue and the other yellow. KC their mother was let outside by the humans to get some fresh air and would be back later in the day. Willy woke his sister Alley who had designs of tiger stripes on her grey coat.

"Alley wake up, let's explore our master's house!" said Willy.

"Can't we sleep a little longer?" she asked.

"Are you crazy? This will be fun!" laughed Willy as he pounced on his sister and wrestled with her.

"Ok, ok! I'm awake," she growled and snapped back at her brother. They stopped wrestling and proceeded upstairs. They were a couple of kittens that loved to play and seek adventures.

The two kittens jumped up from one carpet step to the next, slowly. It seemed to take forever, but eventually they made it to the top and they saw the fluffy surface went on from the staircase. Willy smelled the air and saw a small bowel of chicken meat.

"Hey Alley, our master left us some food, hurry let's get something to eat."

Both of them ran to this area where the bowl of chicken was. The floor was smooth and shiny with lots of weird noises coming from a strange box that had a door and held food. Their mother told them it was the sustenance of all their food and they would be worry free. Their master would take care of them and the box would always have food. Willy started eating first just as Alley got in there to eat some of the chicken meat. Next to the saucer of chicken was a bowl of milk.

"Oh what a kick!" exclaimed Alley as she began licking it up.

"Isn't life great," laughed Willy.

"Yes," answered Alley with a smile.

"What should we do today?" asked Willy.

"I don't know," replied Alley.

"I know what we can do," began Willy.

"We can sneak outside and go on an adventure."

"But aren't we forbidden to go out there?" she asked.

"How are they going to know if we sneak out and make it back before dinner?"

"I don't know," answered Alley.

"Oh come on, are you crazy? It'll be fun," said Willy.

Both kittens hid as the humans walked in; the kittens scuttled out when the door opened. They looked at the tall grass and the trees to see the world was big. Two baby kittens ahead of their years and unaware of how to defend themselves. They immediately ran through the tall grass and tried to catch grasshoppers.

"This is fun!" laughed Willy.

"Yes it is," replied Alley as both cats hopped out of the grass and onto what was a path where the humans would ride strange square objects with circular objects that made a loud noise.

The two kittens ran across the path, into some tall grass and found themselves in a forest. They traveled through a deep ravine where there was running water and hopped on one rock to the next without getting wet. Willy jumped up on a log and began sharpening his claws by rubbing it. Alley turned her head and realized that there was a large creature following them. This other animal was a fox and it was hunting for food.

"Willy, I want to go home!" she cried.
"Would you relax, there's nothing here to hurt us," assured Willy.
Then Alley took off in a run, "we got to go!"

She ran past him as Willy turned his head to see the large animal look at them and then pursue them. They ran quickly with the fox chasing after them.

KC was let in the house and looked for her babies, but they were nowhere to be found. She began to get worried and snuck out of the house through the front door. She sniffed the air, but there was nothing to smell and walked around the pavement while listening for the sound of cries from Willy and Alley. Sheba, the black lab, and peppy, a brown poodle, ran up to KC.

"What's wrong?" asked Sheba.
"My babies are missing and I think they're in danger."
"The outside world is no place for kittens," replied Peppy.
"Sheba can you help me find them? They could be in danger and I need to find them as soon as possible," begged KC.

Sheba began sniffing the ground and right away picked up their trail. KC and Peppy wasted no time and followed the big dog to the kittens. KC's heart beat faster with each passing minute and she hoped that they weren't dead.

They walked through tall grass and a ravine full of water until they came to a meadow with a couple trees. In one of the trees were the two kittens in the branches. On the bottom was a fox and immediately Sheba charged at the fox.

"Leave them alone!" growled the black lab.

The fox turned around to face Sheba and backed away while baring his teeth until KC and Peppy got there. Peppy wouldn't stop barking and KC began to hiss at the fox. The fox looked at the three realizing he was outnumbered and ran away.

"Ok, you can come down from the tree," ordered KC as she watched Willy and Alley climbed down and looked at their mother who wasn't happy.

"What have you to say for yourselves?" asked KC sternly.

"We're sorry," they replied together.

"It was wrong for us to run off without telling you," said Willy.

The animals returned to the house and were happy to be home. KC was relieved that the kittens were alive. After getting a taste of the outside world they were already talking about the next adventure, but that's another story.

The Flesh Beast II: The Sound Of Ripping Flesh

Jamie could hear his own feet running along the floor as well as the sound of his own heart beating faster and faster. It was mid-night and he took a short cut in a maze of tunnels to escape the beast that was hunting him. The red head child with brown eyes snuck into the kitchen to steal some cookies when he heard something whisper, *where's my flesh?*

Jamie remembered the horror stories of what happened to the other children a few days ago. As he kept running through the dark tunnels with a lantern in his hand, he could hear the deep voice of the creature behind him.

"Where's my flesh?" it growled.

Jamie stopped to look back with the lantern and in the distance of the dark tunnels he saw the creature's yellow eyes gleaming at him like a gargoyle. Jamie screamed his head off and started to run again. The boy kept running as fast as he could, but each step he made seemed to move slower and slower.

He could hear the deep breathing of the beast and heard the sound of a roar near his ears. The boy ran up to the open metal grate and climbed up the wooden ladder. He closed his eyes and quickly pushed the huge metallic object with his hands and lifted it up as he crawled out.

"Where's my flesh?" the beast shouted as it grabbed the boy's ankles, bit off both feet and began eating them while holding his ankles.

Jamie screamed, but nobody was coming to his rescue. He felt his legs go numb and the sound of growl through his ears as blood shot out of his mouth and his eyes became still. His body was dragged back under the metallic grate as the flesh beast began to eat Jamie, bone and flesh.

It was dawn and little Barry opened his eyes to see the sun peer in from the window. He was sent to the Insane Asylum Correctional Facility for Boys and Girls for trying to kill his little brother. His parent's didn't know what to do with him because of the reckless swearing and killing cute little animals.

Barry Bates rose out of bed to get ready for breakfast and noticed that Jamie Bogie was not in bed. The black haired, twelve year old ca ca mouth boy got out of bed and looked around. His other friend Steve Lickee was still sleeping. Steve and Barry were best friends, but only met each other for a short time and became twits to make each other look bad.

Barry was into that kind of trouble making and liked it like that. Steve was another trouble maker often involved in picking fights with other kids and swearing. He got sent to the institute for picking on and beating up a fellow student in school for nothing. This blonde hair, brown eyed bully found himself put in the institute by order of the principle of the school in Shellmont.

Amy Quin opened her eyes to see it was morning and she already hated it. Amy hated the asylum and thought Ms. Knealson was a witch. It was her third week in the insane asylum and this blonde hair, intelligent, preteen heard awful stories from many of the students that the flesh beast ate the children and would repeatedly ask *where's my flesh?*.

Amy was brought to the asylum for lying, stealing and fighting with other girls. Amy managed to make friends with Koko, Steve, Barry and Jamie. Her girl friend Koko Strike was brought in for making a hit list to kill other students. When asked why? She said it was for fun and that she wanted to know what it would be like to hunt another human being.

Koko was reported repeatedly for talking about how she liked to wear the color black and that it made her feel closer to her goal of blending with shadows. The psychologist of Shellmont School thought that if nothing was done she would become a slayer.

Of course Koko was just joking around and wasn't serious. The hit list was a list of who to steal money from not to kill, but nobody saw it that way. The twelve year old brown eyed, burnet became good friends with Amy. They were like sisters and shared the same room. Amy woke up to take a shower, got dressed and walked down stairs to meet her friends for breakfast.

Amy, Barry and Steve sat at the table with the other kids as they waited for breakfast. They were quiet and knew the reason why Jamie wasn't at the table. The other kids were busy talking about the day and what they were going to do for the next class. The younger kids got to play all day, but still learned arithmetic, reading and writing.

Then a student came to the table with a tray full of food. He was about twelve, slender with black hair and brown eyes. The boy looked like he was afraid of something.

"Is it alright if I sit with you?" he asked.

The other three students shrugged and Steve spoke up, "sure, we don't care, we're sick of this place."

"Yeah this place is for maggots," replied Barry. "What's your name?"

"My name is Adam."

"Where's Jamie?" interrupted Koko as she looked at Barry.

Barry looked at the twelve year old misfit girl with a distinguished look on his face. It seemed pretty obvious why he wasn't at the table. The dumb kid had to go run around the asylum looking for the flesh beast.

"What are you guys talking about?" asked Adam.

"We're talking about your mom," replied Barry. "She saw me and got excited.

Adam began turning red and looked angry, but said nothing. Barry just looked at him with a cocky laugh and talked to Steve. Adam already didn't like the kid and wanted to beat his brains in, but then the flesh beast popped in his mind. The creature that ate naughty children would enjoy chomping on this maggot mouth pee brain.

"So is this thing for real or is just some kid dressed up in a suit?" asked Barry.
"I don't know? For all I know it could be a polka dot dinosaur singing koombia after it steals kids," said Steve.
"I heard it uses your fingers as toothpicks after each meal," replied Amy as she laughed.
"It does," agreed Adam.
"Yeah, well how would you know?" asked Barry.
"Because I saw it," replied Adam as he watched Barry, Steve and Amy's eyes widened. "I was eight years old and it ate my two friends."
Then all of a sudden something crept up behind Amy and grabbed her waist while yelling, "where's my flesh?"
It was Koko and she unleashed a scream with Amy. All the kids stopped eating and looked at them. The group felt embarrassed and Koko continued to scream.
"Would you shut your blood sucking mouth you dumb dog eat dog whore!" exclaimed Barry.
Then the students continued to eat and carry on their own conversations. Steve and Barry took a deep breath and felt relief that they wouldn't continue to get stared down by the students.
"Where's Jamie?" asked Koko as she laughed in her high pitch squeaky voice.

"Hey I could have choked on my food and died," replied Amy.

Barry set his head down on the table and then raised it, "I got to get out of this ship of fotay maggots."

"He got eaten by the flesh beast," replied Steve.

"So who's going to be next?" laughed Koko

She took an orange began unpeeling it while carefully putting pieces of it in her mouth and sucked the juices. Adam got goosebumps from it because it was exactly how the flesh beast ate his friend Joey.

"Hopefully you," replied Barry.

"Is there a problem?" said a voice.

"No Ms. Knealson everything is fine," replied Steve.

"Good, where's Jamie?" she asked.

"We don't know," answered Steve.

Ms. Knealson looked at Adam as her pupil turned yellow just slightly and then back to black. Adam raised his eyebrows in fear as he remembered the past.

"Are you ok Adam?" asked Ms. Knealson.

"Yes, never better."

"Good," she answered and walked away.

"That lady is a dog dong," whispered Barry.

"Yeah," they all agreed except Adam who turned pale.

"Hey maggot boy," said Barry. "What do you think of her?"

"She's evil," answered Adam.

"Well I think this flesh beast is a joke and I'm going to prove it. Let's all gang up on whoever is behind this and beat them up. Are you in or out?" asked Barry.

"I'm in," answered Adam.

It was dark and all the children were sleeping in their beds. Barry and Steve were awake and creeping by the door in their clothes. They walked into Adam's room to wake him up.

Barry slapped his hand across Adam's face and whispered, "wake up maggot boy."

Adam woke up and rubbed his eyes, "what time is it?"

"It's about a quarter to midnight," answered Steve.

"We got work to do," whispered Barry.

The three went to find Koko and Amy's room. They walked around in the dark halls with candles. Blue light from the moon shined through the windows and gave the hallway an unsettling appearance for Adam.

Adam was scared because it was the same hallway that his friend Joey and Jennifer died in. They carried sticks and knives from the kitchen so they could kill the beast. They were in front of the girls' bedroom door and Barry knocked while the door opened slowly and they came out.

They walked around the hallway, looking and listening for the flesh beast, but all they heard was the sound of the ringing in their ears and the sight of shadows from beyond the candle light.

They came across something quite creepy and Barry lowered his candle to see it was a rat walking in the corner trying to get past them. Then Barry realized that Adam was missing and turned the candle past his friends to see if he was behind them.

"Where's that little maggot?" whispered Barry.
"Who?" asked Steve.
"Adam."
"I don't know?" replied Steve.

"I don't know why we bothered with that stupid little chicken," replied Barry as he continued to lead them.

Adam had wandered downstairs to the grandfather clock. He heard rumors that the flesh beast came out of the clock in search of naughty children. The boy hid next to the book shelf and waited for the clock to strike midnight. Minutes went by and finally the clock struck midnight and made a loud noise. After it was finished, Adam saw something rip through the fabric of air.

It was about eight feet tall with yellow eyes and built like a crocodile, but with the hind legs of a man and a long tail. It had a long, black, greasy mane and grey skin. It opened its mouth to reveal its sharp teeth as they began moving up and down its jaw bone like a chainsaw.

Then the teeth stopped moving as the beast unleashed a roar, similar to a lion and then it said, "where's my flesh?"

The kids walked down the hallway trying to hold their candles from the blowing wind to see where they were going. Suddenly, Barry heard a strange sound in the distance, about fifty feet away. He saw it was something big and its yellow eyes stared at him.

"What is that?" whispered Koko.
"Shut up!" said Barry.
Suddenly, they heard a whisper, "where's my flesh."

Amy freaked out and retreated back to her room screaming and then that's when the beast revealed itself by shouting the question, "where's my flesh?"

Barry watched it get on all fours and charge towards them like a bull. Its mouth opened up as its teeth ran up and down its jaw like a chainsaw.

"Where's my flesh?" it repeated like a broken record.

Barry hit it in the face with a stick, but only made it angry. The flesh beast picked him up as it opened up its mouth while its teeth moved and scared him. Barry pissed his pants and began screaming like a little girl.

Steve ran up behind it and hit the flesh beast in the back with his chimney cleaner which allowed Barry to fall to the ground. The flesh beast turned to Steve and swiped his claw really fast to dis-arm the boy.

The metal weapon used to clean the chimney fell to the floor and rolled away. What Steve didn't realize right away was his right hand was missing. Steve's mouth dropped as the flesh beast smiled and picked up his missing appendage and flung it down the hallway. Then it growled before shouting, "where's my flesh?"

A tear fell down Steve's cheek while he watched the teeth in the creature's mouth up and around each jaw bone faster and faster, but Barry and Koko came to his rescue. That is they tried, but not until the flesh beast stabbed Steve with its right claw and devoured him.

Koko was stabbing the flesh beast with her kitchen knife as many times as possible and shouting, "die, you demon from the underworld!

"Where's my flesh?" shouted the flesh beast, responding to the stabbing by Koko.

Barry got scared and took off, leaving Koko with the flesh beast. He heard the sound of the beast growling and heard her scream. The flesh beast ripped Koko's arm off with the knife and then bit off her head before before ripping the rest of her body apart. The flesh beast looked ahead to see Barry and Amy were getting away. The creature ate Koko quickly and charged after the children after shouting, "where's my flesh?"

Barry and Amy knew of a secret passageway to escape and Amy opened up the metal grate, which was an air vent. They crawled through the air vent quickly to escape the clutches of the flesh beast that was coming for them. Barry looked at Amy and they realized they made a mistake to disbelieve the rumors of the flesh beast.

"I'm scared," began Amy as she hugged Barry.

"Don't touch me! I don't have time for this mushy love crap, its disgusting," declared Barry as he watched her cry.

They both continued to escape, but looked behind to see something in the distance of the narrow corridor, the flesh beast. There was the sound of its loud chattering teeth and its yellow eyes glowing in the dark as it shouted, "where's my flesh?"

Amy screamed as Barry ran. She could already feel the flesh beast's claws de-cloth her and rip her skin apart that would spill the blood all over the floor. Barry didn't care if she was killed as long as he got away.

Barry was in front of Amy and the exit from the hidden passage was right in front of them. He pushed on the metal grate and crawled out to find they were downstairs in the reading area where the grandfather clock was.

Suddenly, Amy started screaming while she crawled from the hole of the secret passageway, "Barry help me, its got me, please!"

Barry heard a loud roar and then the sound of bones being ripped from her while she screamed in pain. A little bit of blood came out of her mouth and then her eyes closed as her corpse was dragged backwards and then devoured followed by the sound of broken bones.

There was a big belch and Barry screamed as the creature poked its head above the metal grate and exited out from the passage way. It licked its lips and claws that had Amy's blood. A young girl's blood who was naughty made the blood sweet and tasty.

Barry screamed even more as it shouted, "where's my flesh?"

Finally, as it caught up with the mouthy ca ca boy who escaped. The flesh beast stabbed Barry in the chest with its claws and lifted him up as he screamed in a terrified cry.

"You've got my flesh!" exclaimed the flesh beast as it opened its jaws wide so Barry could watch its shiny, white, teeth run up and down its jaw bone. Quickly the beast devoured Barry by ripping off his head, arms, legs and sucked out his intestines. Barry died slowly while feeling the severe pain of being chopped up and his organs devoured.

Adam peered down at the flesh beast from on top of the shelving unit above the clock and saw that Barry was gone. With a kick; the grandfather clock fell down on top of the flesh beast and busted into a million pieces. Adam jumped down to the ground and saw that the creature was gone.

"Adam Folkoskee!"

Adam turned his head to see it was Ms. Knealson and she did not look pleased. Ms. Knealson grabbed Adam and they walked into another room filled with grandfather clocks. Adam's mouth dropped and felt scared because the flesh beast came out of just one grandfather clock. Now, in this room he had to deal with hundreds of them.

"I want you to dust and clean every clock or you won't be eating breakfast," she ordered and she left, following the slam of the door.

Adam turned around to look at the clocks and as he picked up a wet towel from the pale nearby and began cleaning. He could hear the whispers coming from each one, "where's my flesh?"

Healing Heart: Love Is Frozen In Time

This is for Kisus.

It started with a phone call from Wes White to Annie Metoxen. He opened his heart after reading a good book about love and relationships that would help him work past his fears of rejection. He read a book and learned that long-term friendships could be turned into loving relationships. Then he thought of Annie and that they could create a life together. The bus ride to Colorado was quiet that evening and he looked at his digital watch as the sunset to see it was a few minutes after eight thirty.

Memories flashed back of when he first met Annie as a teenager. He was fifteen and she just turned sixteen at a barn dance in Wisconsin. He remembered how they met those precious years ago and it was the beginning of their soulmate relationship. She was his soulmate and maybe his future love.

Wes sat in his chair and was busy drawing a heart with a sword stabbed into it. It was an awesome illustration that had flames springing from it with wings. He was almost finished shading it when a friend of the family interrupted him.

"Hey Wes, there's someone who's interested in what you're drawing," said a

*feminine voice and shortly after that Wes looked
up to see it was Belinda, a friend of the family.*

*She directed him to the girl who was
interested in what he was drawing. She sat
across the room and was watching him. The girl
had blue eyes and her hair was black, but
partially dyed red. There was something
peculiar about her that gave him curiosity. Wes
took his illustration and slid it back into his
drawing book.*

*The girl's energy was like a rock, in a
stream, that had been smoothed out with sharp
edges. The surface of her personality was so
soft you could lay your face upon it like a
pillow, but if you turned it sideways you would
cut yourself. Wes ignored his intuition and
gathered his courage to visit her at the table and
she looked at him.*

"Hi, my name is Wes."
"My name is Ann," she replied smiling.

*They continued to talk about their
nationalities and the area of Wisconsin as well
as the barn dance. She didn't know anybody in
the area and was from Hawaii. Wes could see
that Ann was quite a bit taller than him and she
was like an amazonian. She was wearing high
heels and he looked up to her. He was only five
foot seven, but he was still growing and hoped
to reach six foot. They parted ways after the
party, giving each other their address to write
each other.*

Wes smiled with the memory of when they first
met. He didn't realize that it was the beginning to an
unusual friendship. Now that he was on his way to visit,

he wondered where it would lead. The bus ride continued to its destination and Wes continued to smile as he remembered when they reunited as friends in Wisconsin a few years after the first visit.

It was the summer of 1997 and he took a greyhound bus to visit Annie. He could still remember sitting in the bus station and seeing Belinda and Ann walk in as if it was yesterday. Wes closed his eyes as he thought about the visit.

Wes sat in his chair and waited for what seemed to be an eternity. Finally, after ten minutes he saw Belinda and Ann. Annie looked completely different because she lost a lot of weight and her hair was grown past her shoulders to the middle of her back, she looked beautiful.

She reminded Wes of Snow White because her skin was white as snow and her hair was black as night. Her blue eyes captivated his heart and made him wonder what her future plans were.

They said hello and took the ride back to Belinda's house. Ann was quiet in the car, but Belinda kept talking about plans that she had for them.

One of the plans was to go to the House on the Rock. Wes sat in the back seat of the car and was looking at Ann's long black hair. She had her nose pierced on the right side and was wearing a white t-shirt and blue jeans.

Every day there was something new to do, together as friends. They walked up and down State Street by the capital to look in the little gift shops.

One of the memorable moments Wes had was the movie, Species. Wes put his hand on

*hers and caressed it. It was warm and soft and
there was no resistance. He was scared that she
would slide her hand away from him, but she
kept it on the arm of the chair and said nothing.
It seemed that she liked it and touched his hand
back a little bit. It was a lot of fun and Wes
didn't want it to end, but like all good things
they come and go. He faced Ann to give her a
hug good-bye and got on the bus.*

Wes smiled with the flashback that entered his mind, but that was ten years ago and much had happened to his friend from Colorado. He did some exploring on his own on his path to romance and learned things the hard way.

Ann got ahead of him and was going through her second divorce and had a couple of kids. She was happier with the world she created and was looking forward to seeing him.

Wes couldn't understand why he waited so long to get together with her in the first place, but realized that whenever he was single she was seeing someone. Whenever she was single he was seeing someone. Something told him that there was something special about them.

Maybe it would work out and they would be a couple. A couple that would lead into a lasting, loving relationship. Wes felt they were compatible and it would only take the next step for intimacy.

A song emerged on the radio that caught Wes' attention and inspired him with ideas of what could be expressed. It was a song by Amy Grant and her voice was best described as an angel. The song she was singing fit exactly how he was feeling at the moment and it was a song called "I Will Remember You". It made his heart beat faster as the line she sang *our love is frozen in time* entered his mind. It made him wonder if the relationship and the thoughts he was having was one sided or was Ann thinking the same of him. Wes closed his eyes and began day dreaming of his fantasy evening with Annie. A picture entered such mind of her beautiful face looking at him.

Wes sat at the bus station and waited. Ann pulled up in her Kia and smiled. Wes grabbed his book bag and walked outside the station to meet her.

She was wearing a plain shirt with a jean jacket and blue jeans. Her black hair was shoulder length and she looked almost the same as she was ten years ago. Wes gave her a hug and after a few seconds they were both in the Kia. Ann turned on the radio as Wes turned around to see the baby chair in the back seat.

"Where's Seilah?" he asked.

"Seilah is staying at her aunt's house for a couple days and Haden is being baby sat by my cousin Angie."

"It's been a long time," replied Wes.

Ann began smiling, "yes it has."

They turned into a frontage road to a group of apartments. She pulled into her parking spot, put it in park and turned the car off. Wes felt excitement, but also a little scared because he didn't know what to expect.

"We're here," she replied and turned to Wes.

Wes looked around to see the lay out of the grass and trees that were around the building. The apartment looked cozy from the outside and when he turned to look at Ann who was smiling at him. He felt her confidence resonate against him and smiled back.

"It's a nice place," he said.

"Thanks, except for the loud lady upstairs who likes to play her music loud so that my kids can't get any sleep," Ann replied with a light laugh.

Wes didn't say anything as they both got out of the car and walked inside her apartment. Wes walked into the living room and sat on the couch, everything seemed plain. Ann sat on the chair and they looked at each other for a while and smiled.

The days continued uneventful as each night Wes slept on the couch and Ann slept in her bed. Wes got to meet Haden before he left to be with his dad and Seilah played board games with Wes after school.

While Ann went to work, Wes walked around town exploring and walked into a bookstore to read. He enjoyed it, but he kept thinking about Ann and wondered what she wanted for her future.

She was beautiful, cute, funny and always surprising him with activities. He couldn't help but laugh on the phone when she talked about her day. She told stories about her friends and family that was filled with laughter. That's partly how relationships are supposed to be, thought Wes. They're supposed to have lots of laughter, but most of all honesty and communication. They already had the embryo for a great relationship.

The very next day, Wes and Ann spent the whole day together going on nature hikes, watching a movie and making stir fry at her apartment. Seilah was being watched by Angie.

Finally, he couldn't resist and when the food was near finished he walked up behind her. He touched her waist with his hands and caressed the back of her neck with his lips.

He saw a tattoo of a broken heart that was stitched together on the back of her neck and knew she needed healing. He stopped with the romance, but it didn't stop there.

She turned around, looked into his eyes with hers and began kissing him. First on the lips, then on the neck and then she put her hands on his bare arms. He could somehow sense her pain and wanted to heal her heart, but knew that she was the only one that could do that.

Wes slowly and passionately French kissed her as he picked her up with his arms and set her on the counter. He then stopped and watched her smile at him and smiled back while touching her face with his hands.

"I waited ten years for that?" she began. "You could have kissed me when I was at Belinda's house."

"You were talking about marrying your boyfriend and I didn't think you wanted me."

Ann took a deep breath and looked into his eyes as Wes could see she was thinking. Her blue eyes hypnotized him and when she smiled it made him feel weightless.

"Aren't you hungry? We got all this food, don't you like to eat?" she asked.

Wes smiled and felt her hands on his back as he lowered her to her feet again. They sat at the candle lit table and began to eat.

Each bite of the stir fry was delicious. Wes looked into Ann's eyes and could feel the weight in his arms from lifting her. He could see every hugh of her skin that the candle would allow and it was beyond beauty. Wes pulled out a bottle of Brandy and two glasses.

"I would like to propose a toast; to old friends that may never be forgotten," he announced.

Ann sipped her glass of Brandy as Wes did the same. It tasted good and he knew after a few more glasses they would be intoxicated. Maybe he would get lucky to get a dance with her in the living room with the stereo on and have a lot of fun.

"I thought you said you don't drink," she said.

"I don't, unless it's a special occasion," he whispered.

After they were finished they both looked at each other and wondered what would become of them. Ann couldn't help but smile for she had never experienced such a wonderful evening. Wes touched her ankle with his foot and she began to laugh.

"Would you like to dance?" he asked.

She nodded as he watched her get up to turn on the radio. There was a couple songs playing that were too fast to slow dance to, but they didn't care. They just started moving and didn't care if the rhythm was matching to the song. They drew close to each other and destiny seemed to surface as Amy Grant's song surfaced, "I Will Remember You", began playing on the radio and Wes' eyes opened in surprised.

Wes opened his eyes and realized he dozed off and had been dreaming. However, the radio on the bus was playing the same song by Amy Grant again as was in his dream.

He looked out the window and saw that it was morning. He looked at his cell phone for the time. It was a few minutes after eight that morning. In about an hour, the bus would be at the station.

When the bus got to the station, Wes got off and saw that Ann was there. He saw her children as she waved at him. He smiled and waved back as he met with them.

"Did you have a good bus ride?" she asked.

"Let's just say, it was an interesting," he continued to smile as she introduced her children and Wes talked about his bus ride.

"How would you feel about visiting the Garden of the Gods?" she asked while starting her car.

"I like it," answered Wes as they drove out of the city of Denver.

An Angel Visit II: The Act Of Temptation

Rya looked around inside the vacant apartment that was located in Almond. The apartment was clean and there was an agreement with the Landlord to move in. It was the beginning of an adventure to write the follow up to his original story.

The writer put together ideas for his second novel to "An Angel Visit" after settling in into his new apartment. He also moved on with a new girlfriend that he met at Road Way Service and her name was Alyssa.

Alyssa was unlike any girl he went out with, she inspired him to write by encouraging him and complimenting his efforts. She had green eyes, a broad lower lip with dimples followed with curly, black, shoulder length hair. Alyssa had a cynical attitude and a laugh that was very contagious. She described herself as the moon and her older sister was the sun, but for Rya she was his queen. Her white skin was porcelain in color and she looked beautiful when they went outside at night when the moon shined on her.

In this new chapter of life, Rya found new techniques while at work to write the next installment and continue seeing Alyssa. He was busy, day after day, writing and editing but he began illustrating a picture. The piece of paper was blank with only circles of what would be self-portraits.

Rya found inspiration to write the second angel book by reading the bible. He missed Sarah and it had been a few years since the visit and he wondered where she was. Rya began rendering the picture as he thought of his guardian angel.

It was the middle of July; Rya continued when something abruptly growled in his ear. The writer jumped out of his chair and ran out of the apartment. He felt the hair on the back of his neck stand up and wondered what was going on. He looked around and saw nothing in the bedroom, but decided to take a break to think things through.

Days turned into weeks and there were no more episodes. It was evening and Rya was looking into Alyssa's eyes with a smile. It was late at night and the movie they were watching was a fantasy with unicorns, elves and fairies. They were kissing and didn't care about the movie because they already knew it had a happy ending, just as they were going to live happily ever after.

Rya was in love with Alyssa, she made him feel good and they had been together for almost a year. They cooked pizza and talked about what they wanted out of life. She was intuitive, loving and always had something fascinating to talk about. Alyssa was his muse and he was her king; together they were like the sun and the moon.

"So what do you think of this place?" he asked.

Alyssa looked at him and was a little hesitant, "I don't know, your walk in closet is creepy."

"I feel like something is watching me," replied Rya.

"Like what?" she asked.

"Something dark," he continued as he saw his face in her eyes.

"I feel something bad happened there," said Alyssa.

"Like what?"

"I don't know, something evil."

There was a moment of silence and Rya didn't want the conversation to destroy the mood of their romance. He leaned over while they were on the couch and kissed her. They looked at each other while laughing and kissed passionately while listening to the movie they weren't watching.

Then they rolled off the couch and onto the floor. They were laughing and playfully wrestled on the floor like they were a couple of kids.

"Those aren't the rules," she said with a smile as he continued to grind up to her.

Rya looked into her eyes and for a minute couldn't imagine another day without her. She was the one he wanted and their love had surpassed his attraction for Krissy. He knew Alyssa loved him and there was nothing that was going to stand in their way.

"I think you're amazing and I want you, I need you," he whispered.

"I know, I'm the master," she laughed.

"The master?" he asked with a laugh.

"Yes," she laughed as she felt Rya tickle her stomach.

"What do you think you're doing?" she demanded.

"Nothing, I just want to tickle you," he answered.

"Do you think it's going to be that easy?"

"Yes," laughed Rya as he started kissing her and they continued laughing.

After all was quiet he whispered in her ear, "I want to make love to you."

"That's the most beautiful thing I've ever heard," she said and made love to him.

A few months latter in the month of August; Rya put a Celtic CD in the player to relax and concentrate on his work. He played the same song over and over again, but sometimes he would play the entire album because it felt good hearing it.

Rya walked to his car and turned on the CD player to put in the CD, but for some reason it didn't work. Then he walked back to his room and turned on the stereo but the CD wasn't reading either. Rya decided to play it on his computer and realized the Power PC wouldn't even turn on. Rya scratched his head in confusion and went to work without his music.

After work, Rya came home, laid in bed because he was exhausted and slept as the hour grew late. He opened his eyes, after hearing something and was staring at the ceiling in his dark room. He gasped when he saw a black oily object glide down from the ceiling and sat on his chest. Rya couldn't breathe because it was on his chest and he was scared. He felt like he was paralyzed and being drained of energy. He lost consciousness and fell into a deep sleep.

Rya woke up and got out of bed to face the day. The sun was shining through the window. He got up from his bed and walked around, but then turned around to see the bed he was lying on suddenly disappeared. He walked to the refrigerator to find something to eat. Rya opened the door and was shocked to see mold had grown on all his food. He saw maggots and cockroaches crawling on everything.

"Oh my God!" gasped Rya as he slammed the door shut.

Then he noticed his shadow and saw there were shadowy creatures with wings flying around his shadow. The writer looked around the area of where these things should be, but saw nothing. The hair on the back of his neck stood up and his ears began ringing.

Rya heard a young girl crying and the sound of skin on skin rubbing each other, the sound of sex. He followed the sound into the bedroom and heard it in his walk-in closet. Rya opened the door and saw nothing, but somehow knew what Alyssa was talking about.

"What the hell?" he whispered, feeling like someone had sex with an underage girl.

He soon decided to move on and needed to go to work. Rya in the shower and felt the hot water running down the middle of his back. He thought of Alyssa, his two miscellaneous jobs, the angel book and the rent for his apartment.

He wanted to move in with Alyssa if it worked out, get married.

Rya walked outside and started his car and could see it was a beautiful day for the month of August. When he turned the ignition, his CD player was working and it was playing his favorite song. Rya raised his eyebrows in surprise, but knew the morning was dismal.

Rya pulled out of the parking spot with his Ford Contour and began driving down Davis Street. He drove down the street until a blue minivan pulled out in front of him.

"Oh shit!" he exclaimed as he slammed on the breaks, but it was too late and his dream faded in slow motion with a blanket of white.

Rya woke up with a big gasp and rose out of bed. He heard a knock at the door and the doorbell rang. He stumbled out of bed and felt drained, but answered the door. When he opened it there were two well-dressed people standing in front of him. There was a woman and a man looking at him with a smile.

"Hello, we're part of the local church and would like to invite you to attend," said the woman.

Rya smiled, "no that's ok."

"Maybe we should come back later," said the gentleman.

Rya smiled as he closed the door and turned around to look at his apartment, he could feel something dark and sinister, but as soon as he closed the door it subsided. Evil made Rya push away the visitors from the church who wanted to help the writer so they could have their way with him.

The weeks proceeded for Rya with no events, but the occasional car keys or channel changer being misplaced to feeling drained of energy every morning. He called Alyssa to say I love you, but it was never as satisfying as seeing her. She was staying with her parents far away and they talked about moving in together. She was busy working at the convenience store to get money together to buy a car.

Then one night while sleeping in bed, Rya opened his eyes to hear something walking in his room. He couldn't see anything but the sound of ringing got louder in his ears. Suddenly, his eyes were able to adjust to the darkness and within the dark he saw a number of oily figures standing in the wall. One of them was reaching in and out with their hands from the wall.

Rya felt the hair on the back of his neck stand up and his shoulders became cold. His eyes turned to see five sets of red eyes staring at him from the wall where the closet was. The red eyes were glowing with a strange pulse and were watching him. He quickly got up, ran to the door to turn on the light and looked around to see the evil had disappeared. Rya looked around his room and began thinking his apartment was haunted with evil spirits.

The next couple of days were difficult. Rya was restless, sometimes getting sleep and other days barely sleeping at all. There were nights when he didn't want to go home and stayed in his car looking at his apartment, dreading to go in. Then there was an incident of a visit while he was taking a shower. For a split second he looked and thought he saw someone facing him behind the shower curtain. It was a medium build with long, grey, black hair and it didn't look human. It glared at him through the plastic shower curtain and Rya stared back and didn't say anything. He could hear its creepy voice enter his mind; *we want you.* Rya opened the shower curtain and it was gone.

"I don't know how long I can stay here seeing all that's been seen. I've decided to move back home with my parents until I get things figured out." said Rya on the phone with Alyssa.

"I wouldn't want to stay there either," she answered. "I've got something to tell you," began Alyssa.

"What's that?" asked Rya.

"Well, maybe this would be something good for both of us to reflect."

"Like what?"

"I want some space," she replied.

"Some space? So how much space are we talking about two weeks, two months?" asked Rya thinking that they were now breaking up and after everything seemed to go so well.

"I don't know, but I'll call you in two weeks," she answered.

The two parted on the phone but then a few minutes later the phone rang. Rya looked on the caller ID to see it was Alyssa again. He smiled thinking *boy that was quick.*

"Hello," he smiled.

"Is Justin there?" said a voice that sounded like Alyssa.

Rya hesitated, "this is Rya, who's Justin?"

There was a hang up which left Rya angry and thinking what the hell? She was cheating on him, but why? Wasn't he good enough? Was it because he mentioned that he was thinking about moving back home to save money to plan a life with her that made her do this?

Rya was angry and punched the wall and kicked the door as hard as he could, but it wasn't enough to extinguish his rage. He turned off the medium sized TV, ripped the cord from its socket and threw it halfway down the lawn from his door and walked into his room.

The writer turned off the lights and lied down. He was so upset that his stomach hurt and continued to question himself, why? How could this have happened? Why did this happen? She was the one, the perfect one, but she rejected him. The memories trailed in such mind like a full blown theater of their love life and how things went from perfect to a private nightmare.

Rya closed his eyes and concentrated on his guardian angel, Sarah. Sarah was someone that believed in him and would never leave him. She was beyond beauty, strength and confidence which was what he needed right now. He invested so much emotion, love, happiness and trust into Alyssa that he had nothing left.

"Sarah, I need you, please come to me!" he cried, but she didn't come.

It was late and for a few hours nothing happened. Then Rya heard footsteps and saw the oily figures within the walls. Instead of running away from them in fear he prayed to God to help him and noticed the right side of the room turned white. He was so sick of the torment and decided to fight back.

"Please God, forgive me for all the wrong I've done in the world, the pain suffering I have unleashed to the people and the creatures of the past. I implore you to give me forgiveness and love. Please send the angels here to comfort me and protect me from this evil that is in this room," prayed Rya.

He saw Sarah's face in his mind nodding her head to him sternly and felt strength. He turned his eyes and for a moment saw two archangels appear.

They unleashed their power by slaying the demons in the room. One archangel thrust his flaming sword at the demons that charged. The one with the sword stretched his wings out and unleashed a battle cry for the one they were protecting, "he's saved! Now be gone demons!"

"The human is ours!" shouted the leader of the demons, referring to Rya.

Rya watched the leader of the demons sword fight with the archangel that he thought was male and realized it was female with long black hair. It was confusing to tell what sex the archangel was, but Rya realized the archangel was female and the other angel was Sarah.

Sarah was punching and kicking the demons out of the bedroom. Then, just as the black haired angel cut the demon's arm off with her sword, more angels appeared to give protection while chanting in unison like a choir;

La de na fa
La fa da la
No ve na vomace
No ve lee comace
No ve lee vomace
No ve lee succose

The leader of the demons opened his wings and flew away in pain, leaving the angels in the room. Then not to far from the master's departure did the imps and medium sized demons left. Rya realized that the energy in the bedroom felt powerful and and he was energized from what was going on. He looked at the numerous angels that were looking at him with admiration and courage for what he had to face. Rya smiled, but fell into a deep sleep on the bed from the prayer he called for help. He fell into a sleep, a deep trance that furthered his test.

> *Rya found himself walking behind an aberration that could only be described as the devil. It was tall and wore a leather trench coat with a hood over its head. Rya couldn't see its face because he was behind it. He was chained to it and bound with metal clasps around his wrists. They were walking up the sidewalk by the Crystal Water Bridge and Rya looked to his left to see graffiti of two demons on the wall. In seconds they came out of the cement wall and flew around Rya.*

> *"You belong to us," said the first.*
> *"No one has ever escaped from us," said the second.*
> *"You will be ours forever," declared the first.*

> *Rya looked sad and nodded in agreement as they continued on the long walk, but suddenly he turned his head to the left and saw graffiti of a man on the cement wall. He was wearing a white robe and had a beard. He had a white glow around his body and within a second he came out of the wall and stood in front of Rya. The red flaming demons cursed the man who emerged.*

> *"Go away, he's ours," they hissed together.*

> *The man looked at Rya and a smile slowly emerged as he grabbed the chains and*

broke them. Rya was in shock and looked at him as a smile slowly emerged. This man, this stranger, that he never met in his life was Jesus.

"A man once told me, only a fool continues on the path with his eyes closed and does not know where he's going rather than those who open their eyes to see everything and know where they're going," smiled Jesus. Rya smiled and felt like he was looking in the eyes of someone he had known all his life.

He woke up in his room and yawned as he felt life in him again just like in Rice Lake. He felt the positive energy in the room and noticed that everything was white as it was when he first met Sarah. He turned his head to see Sarah with her arms crossed and her wings spread open with a white glow of light resonating from them. She looked as she did before and was smiling at him.

"You have passed the test of temptation, but be aware that you will continue to be tested as you work your way to learning what you came here for," said Sarah.

"What does that mean?" asked Rya.

"People will work on you to get unconditional love, but what they don't realize is that once you're a part of the light you will never have to work that hard again. Unconditional love is free to give and receive," began Sarah. "Don't be troubled with pebbles in your shoes while you walk through life. You will learn to use your mind and avoid relationships that end similar to Alyssa's. Remember what I told you before; if she really was your soul mate she would've come back for you, don't forget."

Rya became quiet as he remembered how it ended and didn't want to go through it again, "will I see you again?"

"Of course," Sarah began. "Just remember, things aren't so simple and you began illustrating me on paper. Finish it and look upon me with inspiration," Sarah smiled and for a minute she was quiet.

"I must go now, but I assure you all is well. Now wake up for the day and live for tomorrow," her voice echoed followed by the sound of a choir and her body turned into a flame of light before vanishing.

Rya woke up; looked around and knew that he was visited by Sarah. He suddenly had a lot of energy and inspiration to continue the angel book. That same day he cleaned his apartment and called his dad.

"Hey dad, I was wondering if I could come back home for a while. Things aren't working out here," he said and after a few minutes of talking he hung up the phone. When he got off the phone, he felt inspired to illustrate his picture.

He looked at his drawing board and saw the angel illustration of Sarah he had started. Every grace of Sarah's face and eyes were sculpted with the touch of his pencil. Then before he realized it the illustration was finished and the doorbell rang. Rya answered it and saw it was his dad.

"Is everything ok?"

"Yes, everything is great," he replied as he felt a knot in his stomach with the memories of kissing Alyssa. He realized he would never forget Alyssa or the love they shared while they were together.

They loaded the truck up and Rya could feel something different with the weather. It was a bright sunny day, but all of a sudden the sky turned black. The wind moved faster as the writer picked up the last few boxes and jumped in the truck to leave.

As the wind picked up, the apartment door opened by itself. Dozens of red eyes stared outside at the truck and oily figures walked towards the doorway. They were looking at the one who got away and saw the black haired archangel grip her sword in its sheath as she and Sarah stood behind the truck. There was a hiss and loud growl, then the door slammed shut.

The Bird That Couldn't Fly

Once there was a penguin named Perry. He lived where it was cold, but Perry didn't care, he liked it just the way it was. Perry the penguin loved to explore; he loved to go on adventures from place to place and visit animals that were nice.

The little penguin loved to take walks. Perry the penguin saw that there was a beautiful river leading to the mountains. He wanted to see the mountains because they looked so beautiful so one day he decided to follow the river to the mountains. Through his journey, Perry lost his way home.

Poor Perry, the penguin, was sad when he could not find his way back. The penguin looked at the shiny stream, white flaky snow and beautiful mountains. Now he was alone, away from his mother, father and sister. How would he ever find his way back?

Mother Pelican flew high in the sky. She was flying by the mountains and was flying over the stream with her giant wings when she saw the sad penguin. Mother Pelican flew to him and asked, "what's the matter dear friend?"

"I am lost and can't find my way home," he replied.

Mother pelican began thinking that the penguin could live with her and the kids. He was a young child and needed a mother, but she realized she could provide that as well as siblings. The penguin wouldn't be alone and she smiled.

"Tell me young friend, what is your name?" asked Mother Pelican.

"My name is Perry," sobbed the young bird.

"Well Perry climb on my back and I will fly you to my home, " she declared.

Perry did and they flew high and well in the great blue sky. The flight by air was scary because they were flying through the sky. Perry was frightened at first, but then became excited. He felt a wave of happiness and felt saved by Mother Pelican.

They arrived at the pelican's nest that was next to the sea. There were two kids the same age as Perry the penguin. Perry smiled at the pelicans and hoped they could be friends.

"Welcome to my home," grinned Mother Pelican.

"These are my two kids," continued Mother Pelican as she introduced her little birds.

"This is Parter Pelican," she said while gesturing Parter to see Perry.

"Well say hello," ordered Mother Pelican.

Parter looked at Perry, "hello," he answered.

The next pelican looked at Perry as well, "hello," he replied.

The pelican gave Perry a very mean look, but stayed neutral whenever his mother looked at him. Perry could tell that he wasn't liked and it was because he was new, innocent and loving.

"This is Philip Pelican," Mother pelican smiled

thinking that the young birds liked each other and would soon live in happiness.

"I must go," said Mother Pelican.

"Go where?" asked the penguin.

"I must go get some food," said Mother Pelican as she flapped her wings up and flew away.

It was quiet and the two pelicans looked at Perry with mean looks. They looked at him as though he was evil and would've been happier if their mother would have fed Perry to the sharks. Then the thought emerged in Parter's mind, what if Perry mysteriously disappeared?

"You can't stay," said Parter.

"No, you can not stay," repeated Philip.

"Why! Why not?" asked Perry as he began to get upset.

"You're different," said Phillip.

"Yeah, you can't fly," added Parter.

Perry the penguin looked sadly at his flippers, "neither can you,"

"We have feathers, you don't!" said Phillip.

"Yeah, so that means you can't fly!" boasted Parter.

"You can't do anything!" laughed Philip hoping that Perry would be sad enough to jump out of the nest and die.

"Oh, but I can do things; I can jump, I can skip, and I can run."

"Can you wink?" asked Philip.

"I can wink," answered Perry as he showed them.

"Can you roll?" asked Parter.

Perry smiled and rolled, "I can roll."

Philip and Parter were surprised of all the things that Perry could do, but Philip was mean and wanted to make Perry miserable because Perry was different.

"Can you fly?" asked Philip.
"Well no, but-" squeaked the penguin.
"Ah ha you can't fly, you can't be here, nope nope nope," laughed Philip the pelican as he felt his master plan fall into place.

Perry the penguin was sad because he could not fit in. Mother pelican came back home to the nest with food. Everyone feasted on fish, but Perry still felt sad and worked hard to hide his pain. Not even Mother Pelican could tell what had happened.

It was night and the baby pelicans were asleep keeping each other warm. Perry was huddled in the corner by himself shivering from the cold wind. Mother Pelican couldn't understand why Perry didn't want to be around Parter or Philip. The baby pelicans were so nice and wonderful to be around.

"Come and keep warm with Philip and Parter, become part of our family!" she insisted.

The baby pelicans did not say anything, but they stared at Perry with coldness. They hated the penguin and wanted him to disappear. They did not want their Mother to know that they despised him. They thought only about how they would rid themselves of Perry and have their mother to themselves.

The night was cool with the birds resting. A wind storm came and suddenly, without warning, Parter was swept out from the nest and into the water.

"Help, help," he cried.

Mother Pelican woke up to the cry, but because the wind was so strong she could not fly. Mother

Pelican began to cry because she could not save Parter.

"I can save him!" smiled Perry the penguin.
"You can't fly, the wind is too strong!" cried mother Pelican.
"Oh, but I won't fly! I can't fly!" said Perry as he gave Philip a dirty look.
"Then what are you going to do? How can you save Parter?" asked Mother Pelican.

Perry the penguin jumped into the water and glided in a flight below the waves and wind of the storm to where he saw Parter's head. The water was cold, but once inside he felt warm and complete like the fish and seals. Perry the penguin grabbed hold of Parter who was coughing up water.
"Help help!" gasped Parter.
"It's all right Parter! I'm here" declared Perry as he grabbed hold of his wing and swam to shore.
Mother Pelican ran to the shore and held both birds in an embracing hug, "are you alright?"
"Thank you so much," she said to Perry the penguin.

The birds walked back to the nest as the storm ended and the sun rose. Perry watched Parter hug his brother and Mother Pelican realized Perry was gifted. She also heard her stomach whine and had to get food.
"Well I must be off to get food," said Mother Pelican as she lifted her wings and flew away. It was silent after that and the pelicans looked at Perry. Perry became scared because the last time he was alone with them they were mean to him. A gulp went down the penguin's throat as he expected the worst.
Philip walked over to Perry with his wing placed on Perry's shoulder, "Perry we were wrong about you, you can fly."

"Yeah, just differently," added Parter.

"Is there any way you can forgive us?" asked Philip.

"Of course, I forgive you," replied Perry as a smile emerged.

Mother Pelican returned home shortly with some fish. Each of her kids ate the fish in one gulp and she was happy. She watched the trio play and laugh as she sat and rested.

Perry hadn't had this much fun before and didn't want it to end. He was happy, but became lonely when he thought about his own family and his own siblings. Perry missed his family and Mother Pelican knew that he had to go home. She had secretly found Perry's home when she went looking for food.

"Ok, everybody it's time to say good bye," she said.

"Why?" asked Parter.

"Yeah, why can't he stay?" asked Philip.

"Perry must go home," said Mother Pelican.

"But why," said Parter.

"Because he belongs with his own family," said Mother Pelican as she watched Perry smile and looked happy to go home.

They flew and finally landed on familiar grounds. Mother pelican gave Perry a hug good-bye and soon Perry was left on a warm trail to his family. It was home to him and he liked it, just the way it was.

The Magician's Family

Within the boundary of the Crescent Kingdom, near Everlow Forest, lived a family called the Coopers.

They lived alone and away from society because they enjoyed their privacy.

Mother Maria and Levi had three children; Ryu nineteen, Andrea sixteen and Tiffany fifteen. The siblings looked alike, but Ryu was three inches taller than Andrea with shoulder length black hair and brown eyes. Andrea had brown hair and brown eyes and Tiffany had light brown hair with eyes to match. The girls were nearly five foot eight three inches shorter than Ryu and his father. They worked together as a family to provide for one another.

Levi farmed the land and traded with other people. Maria cooked and mended clothes for the children. Ryu watched the house while his parents were bartering and trading goods until the day they went to Castle Crescent.

There were people everywhere in the city square. Farmers were trading chickens or fresh meat for pitch forks and shovels. Others were selling animal hides of tigers, lions and elk to be made into rugs or blankets.

Maria came across an old peddler selling books, dream catchers and paintings of nature. He was a jolly old man with dark brown eyes, a white beard, mustache and long white hair that was in a ponytail, down the middle of his back. When he stood up he looked tall, nearly six foot, and robust which was strange because he looked decrepit.

"Hello, do you have anything to trade?" she asked.

"Would you trade paintings or animal hides for your wheat and butter?" he asked.

"Sure, but I'll have to come back with the butter," replied Maria as she walked away and then turned to see the peddler stare at her. A smile emerged as she turned around and march to Levi's horse to get the butter.

Once she returned, they talked about the day and business of trading in the kingdom. Maria felt like he was a good man because he gave her confidence to do anything. She was magnetized to his spirit and wanted to do something more out of life.

"I used to be a magician and worked for King Marvin of Jaydon," replied the magician. "My name is Thomas Luck."

"Maria Cooper," she introduced and they shook hands.

"I'm a great healer and ran a business with my associates until I was wrongfully accused of something I didn't do," replied Thomas.

"Oh how awful," said Maria.

"I think everything is going to be different now that you're here."

"Why?" she asked.

"Because The Burning Bush told me that a lovely woman who gave me wheat and butter would be the one to help me continue my business," smiled Thomas.

"Wow, that sounds exciting," replied Maria.

"I imagined your daughters are proud to have a mother as beautiful as you?" asked the magician.

"How did you know I have two daughters?" she asked and watched the jolly old man crack a grin.

"I'm a prophet and a great healer, I can take away a person's pain, make dreams come true and I feel that I need to take away the pain in your family," declared Thomas.

Maria felt relaxed as though he put a spell on her. Suddenly, Levi walked over to visit; Maria awoke from her trance and found her husband next to her.

"This is Thomas Luck, he's a magician that worked for the king. He's also a healer and wants to heal our family."

"Great, now can we go home?" asked Levi.

"Honey can't we stay and talk?" asked Maria.

"Our kids are expecting us back by nightfall and I told Ryu I'd be back to get started on the wood pile."

"Chopping wood is good exercise," replied Thomas. "It's good for the spirit and heals the soul," he continued as Levi looked at him strangely.

"All right," replied Maria and the couple left, but Thomas smiled and winked at Maria when she turned her head to look at him.

Days later, Ryu and his father chopped wood and mended the yard. Andrea and Tiffany were busy knitting baskets and quilts to sell at the town square.

Everything was in order and Maria had the impulse to see Thomas again. She wanted to learn why The Burning Bush chose her to help Thomas with his business.

Levi and Maria started making trips to the castle to trade goods and make friends. Thomas talked about philosophy with Levi and Maria, which made them feel important and needed. He told them about his adventures as a traveler and playing in concerts with his wooden guitar. He talked about how he got to meet Lion Ascend and many other great kings. The couple were astonished and thought Thomas was great, but Thomas avoided to answer the question of what he was wrongfully accused of that got him kicked out of the Kingdom of Jaydon. Eventually, Maria talked Levi into allowing Thomas to move into their home.

The wagon pulled up to the house and Thomas jumped out of the wagon like an excited five year old boy. The magician began pulling a few things from the wagon that were important. Levi wasn't happy about having Thomas live with them, but Maria wanted to start her business of becoming a healer like Thomas.

Ryu, Andrea and Tiffany got to meet Thomas and didn't know what to think. Ryu only knew him from stories that his mother shared and they thought he was a hundred years old by the way he looked. Maria arranged to have Thomas move into the vacant bedroom in the basement and the whole family helped him move in, except Ryu.

They ate dinner together with Thomas and listened to him talk about his adventures. Ryu noticed that Thomas was telling his parents what to do and criticized the way they set the table. It was a family tradition to thank their mother for creating the good food, but Thomas said that they should be praying to The Burning Bush for the food that was being served.

"I used to be the king's magician, I slayed dragons and explored lands far in the sea," declared Thomas.

"Wow that sounds exciting! Do you have anything to show us?" asked Ryu.

"Show?" asked Thomas surprised to the question.

"Yeah, you know, like a dragon tooth or a treasure of the far away land you've discovered?" asked Ryu.

"Uh no, but I also climbed great mountains, visited The Burning Bush and spoke to Lion Ascend," continued Thomas.

"What did they say?" asked Andrea.

"I can't tell you," replied Thomas.

"Why?" asked Andrea

"Because it's a secret," declared Thomas.

"I'm going to be a knight and slay dragons," declared Ryu.

"I did that for a time, but like everything else I got bored with it and was interested in saving the princess from other suitors. I didn't like slaying dragons because it kept me from my woman," said Thomas as he noticed Ryu got quiet and just looked at him.

"I want to be a singer," said Andrea.

"I used to sing for large groups of people and got paid millions of gold coins. It was a lot of fun, but like everything else I got tired of it," smiled Thomas as he watched Andrea glare at him and give him a dirty look.

"My advice is that you should look for a good man to marry and pop out babies," Thomas continued.

Maria and Levi started laughing and so did Tiffany. Ryu looked at his sister realizing it was just a joke, but it wasn't that funny. He could already tell that Thomas was a liar, a hypocrite, a phony and a two-bit crook.

"So can you sing to us one of your songs?" asked Andrea.

"I would if I could remember them," laughed the jolly old man.

Andrea looked at her father who was puzzled, but said nothing and then she asked, "you've traveled the land, sang to huge numbers of people and you can't remember your own music?"

"I will but later," replied Thomas.

"I'm going to be a trapeze artist and work in the circus!" said Tiffany.

Thomas looked at her and laughed, "I did that as well and played with the gorillas, lions and bears, but after a while I got tired of it. You should stay home and be a good little polygamous house wife," said Thomas as he watched Tiffany get quiet and look away.

The night continued after the children went to bed. Ryu dreamed about his anima that lived in the land of Zha and had written to him for nine months. Andrea thought about her suitor who lived in the town of the Crescent Kingdom. Tiffany had nothing to dream except how depressed she was about how Thomas made her feel.

Thomas sat at the table and drank wine from his crystal goblet provided by Maria. Thomas looked at the two fine folks as they looked at him. It was getting late and a big day was to come.

"So tell me, why did you move out here in the country and not closer to the Crescent Kingdom?" asked Thomas.

"We don't feel it's necessary to move to a town full of people that get in our business," replied Levi.

"Besides we get a lot of alone time as a family and the kids love it here," answered Maria.

"Does Ryu have a girlfriend?" asked Thomas.

"Not exactly, he's been writing to this girl from another country, why?" asked Maria.

"Well, I think she just wants to be with him to get pregnant and become a citizen of the kingdom."

Maria and Levi looked at each other then Maria asked, "what about our two daughters? What do you see in the future for Andrea and Tiffany?"

Thomas groaned as his left eyebrow rose, but soon he rubbed his hands together to answer, "Andrea has a boyfriend you don't like and what I see is Tiffany having lots of children. Actually, I see a lot of babies in your lives. Are you planning to have more children?" asked Thomas as he watched Maria and Levi look at each other surprised and then at Thomas who winked at them.

"How did you know that?" asked Maria.

"I know everything. I'm one of The Burning Bushes' prophets," he said as he took a drink from the wine and smiled.

They noticed he only had four teeth in his mouth. They noticed it before, but didn't pay attention. It seemed suspicious and they wondered why a guy who was so successful could let himself lose so many teeth.

"What happened to your teeth?" asked Levi.

"It comes with old age," answered the magician as he closed his mouth and continued to smile.

"Well, I think we should call it a night," said Levi as he got up.

"You're absolutely right dad," said Thomas as he rose up and went to go to sleep.

Levi and Maria were in their rooms getting ready for bed. Thomas was in his room lying in bed, waiting to go to sleep. Levi didn't say anything, he had a strange look on his face and Maria knew something wasn't right. They were both lying in bed and Levi was staring at the ceiling.

"What's wrong?" she asked and still got no reply. "You've been very quiet since Thomas got here."

Levi turned his head and got up from the bed, "I don't think it was a good idea to have him live with us."

"What do you mean?" she asked.

"The guy's a queer! I don't want him living here," demanded Levi.

"He gave up his life as a merchant to start our business," said Maria.

"I'm not throwing him out of the house simply because you think he's a queer."

"How do you know he's done half the things he claims? Anybody who claims they're a great musician, prophet and smash the dreams of our children are usually con-artists."

Maria was quiet and the conversation ended without a rebuke. The candle was blown out and they went to sleep. What they didn't realize was that Thomas was listening outside their door and began to smile before returning to bed.

The next day was followed by weeks of Thomas being in the spotlight. He cooked for the family every day and night. He was a jolly old man that loved to wash the dishes, cook chicken and sweep the floor.

Levi and Ryu helped Thomas build wooden benches that would be used in the business to massage customers and get paid. Maria was excited and so was Tiffany. Levi and Maria sat at the table with Thomas to talk about how they were going to get customers and heal them.

Thomas claimed that he could hypnotize people and heal their mind from the damage of the outside world. The magician seemed to be an alright kind of guy and Levi dropped his guard. Tiffany and Andrea seemed to like him; after all, he did pull out the acoustic guitar and played a few songs.

They decided to get hypnotized, but Ryu was the only one that distrusted Thomas and was left un-hypnotized. He saw something vile and destructive about the magician.

Ryu walked into the kitchen with a letter from Reenah, the love of his life. He saw Thomas washing dishes and humming a tune. He had his long white hair tied back into a pony tail and it stretched past his shoulders to the middle of his back.

"Have you seen my mom?" asked Ryu.

Thomas turned around and smiled, "your mom is outside with your dad building the massage tables for my business."

Ryu left outside to see them working on the tables. They looked like mid-evil trap devices and Ryu began scratching his head, "mom, I met this girl from across the ocean and I'm in love with her. Can she stay with us for a week?"

"Thomas says that she's using you to become a citizen in this country and she'll try to get pregnant. I don't want her over here and besides you haven't been nice to Thomas. You need to accept him in our household," demanded his mother.

"And if I choose not to?" asked Ryu.

"Then you're no longer part of our family,"

"This isn't fair!" yelled Ryu. "Isn't my happiness worth anything compared to that demon!"

"He's a jolly, old, man who knows a lot about the world!" exclaimed Maria.

Ryu left and slammed the door behind him to retreat to his room. He wrote a letter to the love of his life, but he already knew that Reenah wasn't going to want him.

Ryu could see the jolly old man clapping his hands and jumping all over the bedroom, laughing hysterically. The worst thing about this situation was that Thomas never proved who he was because nobody from his past knew him.

Thomas finished washing the last dish while humming another tune with his mouth closed and walked outside to see how his massage tables were looking. The tables were just about finished and the last metallic restraint was screwed into the thick wooden frame.

"I heard a lot of commotion with Ryu, what happened?" asked Thomas.

"Oh nothing, he wants his friend from the land of Zha to come over, but I told him there was no chance of that happening and I told him that you said it wasn't ok."

Thomas nodded, "he's going to try to take control, you should throw him out of the house before it's too late."

Later that night, Thomas made supper and poured Brandy on the chicken to give it taste while he was cooking potatoes and gravy. The whole family didn't understand why Ryu was against Thomas being at the house.

Maria walked to his bedroom, "Ryu, will you join us at the table?"

"I'm not coming to the table to pray with a man who claims to be doing the work of The Burning Bush when his intent is to destroy our family!" declared Ryu and heard her footsteps leave the door.

That night Ryu fell into a deep sleep, a state of a trance, where his soul escaped to the dream world. The house seemed cold and empty with no love and sense of purpose. The household changed ever since Thomas took control and nothing was going to be the same.

The house was dark inside and Ryu lit a candle to see where he was going. Everything was dirty, disorganized and cobwebs filled each corner of the house. He came across one of the massage tables with Tiffany lying in it pregnant. She was restrained with a piece of leather material tied around her mouth to the head board that tied her head to it. Her legs as well as her arms were restrained a part and she was naked.

"What the hell is this!" exclaimed Ryu as he unfastened the leather around his sister's mouth.

"You've got to stop him, he's evil!" exclaimed Tiffany.

"Hush," replied Ryu. "Where's father?"

"He killed him so that he could have us to himself," cried Tiffany.

"I'll be right back," ordered Ryu.

"Please don't leave me!" she cried.

Ryu walked around the house and finally came across his parent's bedroom and heard moaning inside. Ryu opened the door to see Thomas having sex with his mother and sister, Andrea. Except it was a dreadful sight. Both of their bodies were merging together into one body. It was like they were both connected from their shoulders, hips and legs and couldn't come apart.

"Leave them alone! shouted Ryu.

Thomas was a hairy old man who turned his head to look at Ryu and gave him a wink, "I can't, they belong to me!"

Ryu watched as the magician let out a snarl while wings of a bat opened up from his back. Then Ryu realized that Thomas wasn't a magician at all but a fallen in disguise, a fallen that destroyed his family and a chance to fall in love with Reenah.

"They're going to supply me the army to conquer my enemies in the world!" he declared as he got up and charged after Ryu. He unleashed a snarl and a loud unbearable scream.

Ryu woke up from the nightmare and wiped the sweat from his forehead. He had never had a nightmare as vivid as this one. The young man looked out his window to see it was daylight. He got out of bed; walked out of his room to see a piece of paper telling him to get out of the house today and that he wasn't wanted. Ryu's stomach turned as he remembered her promise that they would remain a close family no matter what.

Now, the only reminder he had of her was how much of a bitch she was for doing this. He closed his eyes and wiped his cheeks as he heard the torment of yesterday. When he reopened his eyes, he tried to think about what he was going to do next.

His face turned red and he took the letter with him. He walked into the kitchen but it was empty. Then he walked outside to see his sister and father working on the diabolical machines that Thomas claimed were for massaging customers.

"There's something wrong here," replied Ryu.

"Oh, what's that?" asked Levi.

"Why are you and my sisters building these ridiculous tables when Thomas the magician should be doing it himself?"

"We're all helping out with your mom's business so we can get rich," he smiled.

"Oh, is that what Thomas says?" asked Ryu.

"Yeah, Thomas has done everything! He knows everything!" replied Levi.

"You've got to be kidding me!" yelled Ryu and watched Levi laugh.

"Oh, come on, can't you take a joke? He'll be moving out in a little bit!" laughed his father.

"Yeah right, that's why mom nailed this letter on my door telling me to get the hell out!" Ryu replied as he held up the letter and watched Levi walk over to read it.

"I didn't think she was going to do this," he said.

Before Ryu could say another word, his mom walked outside. She put her hands on her waist and looked at her son as though he was dead weight. He could tell she had no tenderness and became a cold, evil mother. Just like the corpse of death; maggots, worms and other parasites sprouted from the ground from each step she made.

"Did you get my letter?" she asked.

"Yes!"

"I want you out of the house because you haven't been nice to Thomas."

"Who in the dog eat dog world cares about Thomas. He's a fallen, a saddest, con-artist, queer, family wrecker and an old hag," replied Ryu.

"You see, that's the kind of language that's unacceptable to me and for Thomas,"

"So is Thomas the one making all the decisions around here? Is he the one who decided to have me exiled?" demanded Ryu as he got no reply. "You know what? Screw this! You're a whore and Thomas is your pimp. As far as your massage business goes, it's going to the dogs!" exclaimed Ryu as he climbed on his horse Bronco and left.

The young man traveled north-east and paid no attention to where he was going. Finally, he stopped by the Magic River and spent a couple hours calming down to get some clarity.

He realized that Thomas worked in the Kingdom of Jaydon as King Marvin's magician. Surely the king would help him with this problem. Ryu climbed on Bronco's back and they traveled to the Kingdom of Jaydon to get help.

Ryu rode through numerous forests and mountainous terrain until finally he traveled to a plateau where he saw the castle and proceeded to learn the truth.

Maria helped her daughters and husband polish up the massage table. She was glad that Ryu left because Thomas told her that her son would try to take over their lives and cause distress. She looked at her husband who was quiet and looked disappointed. Her daughters were also quiet.

"Why are you guys quiet?" she asked.

"Nothing we're just trying to figure out why you threw Ryu out of the house when you told us many times before that we're a close family and you want us around?" asked Andrea.

"I do want a close family; Ryu is old enough to live on his own and besides he wasn't doing anything around the house. All he did was eat us out of house and home and be mean to Thomas," replied Maria.

"Mother, you traded in your only son for a homeless man!" said Tiffany.

"Don't talk that way! Thomas has done a lot for us. He's going to teach me how to hypnotize people and heal them just as he does, which is more than what Ryu has done for the last eighteen years," replied Maria as she heard silence from her daughters and left to find Thomas.

Maria walked back into the house and found Thomas cleaning the butchered chicken and humming to himself. He turned around to see Maria and the jolly old man light up with a smile. He knew what had happened because he heard everything from inside the house and now that Ryu was out of the way he could take complete control of the family. He could really warp everyone's mind; make them do things for him and live like a king.

"So how did it go?" asked Thomas.

"I told him to leave and he left," said Maria.

"Yeah, he's too old to be living at home. Anyways, he should be married and living in his own house," replied the magician as he smiled revealing his four teeth.

"He said terrible things about our business."

"Like what?"

"He said it won't go anywhere and called me terrible names!" cried Maria.

"Oh, don't cry Maria. He's wrong about you and he's nothing, but a bum. He's wrong about the business because now that he said it won't go anywhere it will go even further. He's just saying that out of fear because he doesn't want to believe it. He's the real problem why you haven't been able to do anything because he keeps taking away family values from you to serve himself. He's nothing, but a worthless bum who's been sucking off you," said Thomas as he held her close and waited a few minutes to go by.

"Are the massage tables ready?" asked Thomas.

"Yes," she answered and looked into his eyes.

"Good, have them brought to the back of the house and I'll be there after I get this chicken in the pot."

Maria left and walked back outside to the massage tables and helped move them to the back of the house. Thomas sneered and put the chicken in the pot while imagining how he was going to dominate these women. He had everything going as planned for his new family.

Ryu charged quickly on his horse to the gates of Jaydon and stopped at the entrance. The soldiers stopped Ryu in his tracks and pointed their swords at him. Ryu held up his hands for them to see and one of them searched him for weapons.

"What is your business with the king of Jaydon." spoke the first one soldier.

"I need to see the king, it's dire."

"What is it that's so dire?" asked the second.

"I need to ask the king about Thomas Luck, the magician that served him many years ago!"

"I'll escort you," said the first soldier as Ryu got off his horse and followed the soldier inside the gate to the throne room.

The magician walked to the back of the house and checked out the contraptions. They were built well and he touched the metallic restraints and knew the inevitable was to happen. Maria waited patiently to hear what he had to say and hoped that they were in good standing.

"Why do we need restraints on the massage tables? Aren't the customers supposed to be relaxed while we massage them?" asked Maria.

"The restraints are to keep the customer from injuring themselves and keep their back straight," began Thomas as he kept looking at the contraption.

"Can you lay down in it so I can make sure that it works?" asked Thomas as he watched.

Maria hesitated at first, but when he smiled she proceeded.

"Trust me, it's only for a second to make sure everything is broken in," replied Thomas.

Maria sat in it and watched Thomas slowly set her ankles in the metallic holders and tightened it like a vice. He then did the same with her arms and wrists. It felt uncomfortable, but when she felt the thick leather strap over her forehead and another one over her mouth with an apple she got scared and squirmed.

"Well, I think it works!" declared Thomas as he smiled and looked at her. "What's the matter? You think I did all this just to massage people's butts for a living? I'll be back with your two daughters and they'll help me test the other two," laughed Thomas as he left hearing Maria crying and trying to scream through the apple.

"Thomas Luck is a fallen," began King Marvin as he tried to think of what else the fallen had tried to do. "He tried to take over my kingdom and my crown by breeding with my handmaidens and raising a fallen race to overthrow me. We killed the baby fallens and went after him, but we weren't able to kill the bastard."

"He's taken my family hostage" replied Ryu. "He came across as being a prophet of The Burning Bush and claimed he knew it all."

"Yeah, he said the same to me and my faithful subjects. I won't be joining you, but I will give you weapons to kill him," replied the king as he signaled for the guard.

Ryu suddenly saw something remarkable in the throne room. It was a golden sword in the hands of a statue depicted as a man.

"Wow what's this?" he asked as he walked over to the statue holding the sword.

"It's the demon slayer's sword," said King Marvin as he joined him. "It's called The Demon Stinger and it's never met its match. It kills demons, fallens, gargoyles, dragons, serpents, bats and other demonic creatures including shadow builders."

"I need it! Can I use it to kill Thomas?"

"No, I'm afraid not," said the king. "Don't worry I have other weapons that can kill the fallen. This weapon requires training to be a demon slayer, before you can wield it. Come I'll show you to your weapons," said King Marvin as he led the young man to the armory.

Ryu was given a crossbow with a huge number of silver arrows, holy water, a silver sword in its sheath and shield. Now the young man had tools to slay the fallen and he could envision himself standing over the corpse of the dead Thomas. Ryu held the handle of his sword and looked at the blade before looking at the king.

"Thank you my lord," bowed Ryu.

"Now go and kill the beast," encouraged the king.

"I would like to return to receive the training to become a demon slayer," said Ryu.

"Return if you're defeated and I'll have my mentors give you training to slay the fallen."

Thomas Luck dragged both daughters by the hair to the contraptions and transformed into the fallen. First the dark lavender wings ripped through his shirt; he grew to about seven feet tall but was capable to grow eight feet and his hairy body ripped through his clothing.

"You're a bit stubborn like your brother, but I'll teach you little whores about manners, once I get you strapped in!" exclaimed Thomas with a rough raspity voice.

The girls screamed in horror as they saw the magician's true appearance. He beat them senseless with his fist so they couldn't run away. Once he strapped them into the contraptions, he tightened the restraints and spread their legs apart so he could get easy access into their gorge.

"Do you have any last words?" he sneered.

"Where's our father?" cried Andrea.

"I don't know, I'm sure he's hanging around here somewhere!"

"What have you done with our mother?" asked Tiffany.

"Oh, don't feel bad! She's right there!" laughed Thomas.

"Let us go, this hurts!" cried Tiffany.

"If you think that hurts wait until you give birth to my children!" laughed the fallen as he started to get an erection from looking at them.

Both Tiffany and Andrea screamed as loud as they could. They screamed even louder when the magician revealed the size of his erected trunk. Tiffany and Andrea could see a big grin on Thomas' face.

"Ewe gross!" they cried.

He touched their legs with it as he started to get excited and penetrated Andrea with the swing of his waist. He grabbed her legs and with each thrust he heard her scream in terror. He was getting enjoyment from hearing them cry and after hours of never ending rape. He achieved his objective and watched Andrea's belly inflate slowly.

"Oh, now that I'm finished I've got to move on with the next one," smiled Thomas as he watched Andrea sob and breathe deeply. She watched her diaphragm get bigger and screamed, "what the hell is this!"

Thomas smiled as he penetrated Tiffany and plowed his way through her like there was no tomorrow. Tiffany screamed in pain because she was fifteen and smaller than her sister, but Thomas would make sure she would be big and loose for the hours to come.

Ryu traveled quickly through the night and it seemed it was taking forever to get home. He kept hope that he would get back in time to stop the magician from destroying his family. Time was of the essence; he wiped the sweat from his forehead and kicked his legs against his horse to run faster.

"Come on Bronco, let's move faster boy!"

The fallen was busy thrusting each woman as fast as he could because he knew there was little time to get his revenge with the Kingdom of Jaydon. Each woman gave birth to five baby fallens that slowly came out of their wombs. They were big babies that weighed twelve pounds.

"Stop! I can't take it anymore!" screamed Tiffany.

"I've got a confession to make" began Thomas as he continued his intercourse with Tiffany. "Most of the women that bare my children die after the sixth one. It's kind of a curse I've had, but I've been fortunate and a few have had up to twenty before the woman kicks the bucket!" he unleashed his jolly old laugh.

Ryu entered the property; he saw a bomb fire and eighteen little fallens dancing around with a big fallen. Ryu got angry and raised his crossbow up as he charged and shot as many of them as possible, but most escaped with Thomas by flying away.

The next morning Ryu kneeled down to the graves of his family. His father was hung, his mother and sisters were dead from multiple child births. He was no longer a peasant, he was the demon slayer.

The Boy and His Rat

Jared woke up in his bed after having a dream of school. He hated school and was thankful it was Saturday. Everyone would make fun of the blonde haired little boy with brown eyes for having a rat. The teacher thought it was disgusting and was against the idea of Jared bringing it to the school for show and tell. The rat did tricks and in return Jared would rub its belly.

The nine year old boy smiled while closing his eyes as he thought of Zander, his pet rat. His rat was cool, it was the size of a medium dog and he knew that it loved to have its belly rubbed when it would lie on the ground. He would take it out on walks around the neighborhood. He would walk it past his neighbor Mr. and Mrs. Pootang who lived on the left side of the house. Then there was the neighbor across the street, Mrs. Muffit, who hated rats and chased after them with the broom.

Across the street from Mrs. Muffit were kids from the Porticuss house and next door were the Padikins, they would try to kill his rat by having their dogs attack it. The dogs were mean and almost killed Zander if it wasn't for Jared who kicked the dogs away. Jared loved Zander and kissed the rat's paws before rubbing his belly.

It was morning and Jared woke up to find Zander had escaped from his cage. Jared looked under his bed and then the closet. He then went down stairs to where his mother was busy cooking breakfast. His mother was busy flipping pancakes, eggs and didn't care about her son's rat.

"Mommy, mommy I can't find Zander, what should I do?" he asked.

"I don't know," she answered and was busy making breakfast.

Jared left his mom and talked to his dad who was busy watching TV. He hoped the Zander was ok and wasn't hurt.

"Daddy, daddy Zander escaped his cage and I don't know where he went. What should I do?" said Jared as he noticed his father was too wrapped up into the television to care what his son was saying.

"Go and ask the neighbors if they've seen him," said his dad.

Jared decided to walk outside and walked to each neighbor's house to ask if they had seen his pet rat. He first went to Mr. and Mrs. Pootang's house which was next door. Jared pressed the door bell and Mrs. Pootang answered the door and looked at the boy.

"Yes," she said.

"My pet rat got out of his cage. Have you seen him? He's about the size of a dog and loves getting his belly rubbed."

"That disgusting creature dug up my lily garden and killed Fluffy, my little cocker spaniel. It went across the street before I could get a baseball bat to kill it."

Jared looked at her scared and said, "you didn't try to catch it?"

"Catch it? Are you crazy? Those things are pests and deserve to be killed. Why can't you be a normal child and get a dog or a cat?"

"Zander is my pet! I had him for a long time when he was small. He loves getting his belly rubbed," replied Jared.

"Get a dog!" yelled Mrs. Pootang and she slammed the door in Jared's face.

The nine year old then walked over to the next house, which was the Porticuss and knocked at the door. A boy named Tommy answered the door and looked at Jared, "what's up?"

"My pet rat got out of his cage, have you seen him? He's about the size of a dog and loves getting his belly rubbed."

"Your rat ate our little chi wow wow and our French poodle and made a mess out of my mom's rose garden, rats deserve death."

"Please don't, he's very important to me. I taught him tricks like how to play dead," cried Jared.

"I'll be teaching it how to play dead," smiled Tommy. "With a bullet, now get lost twerp."

Jared walked to the next house, which was the Padikins and knocked on the door. A man answered the door and looked at Jared, "what can I do for you guy?"

"My pet rat got out of his cage. Have you seen him? He's about the size of a medium sized dog and loves getting his belly rubbed."

"Uh huh," replied the man.

"Have you seen him?"

Suddenly, there was the sound of a shot gun from the next door neighbor. It was a ninety-six year old lady named Mrs. Ethel.

"God forsaken pest chewed all the wiring in my house and I got the bastard for making me miss my soaps!" she yelled.

"No," cried Jared as he ran over to his rat and kneeled down to it. The rat was dead, its tongue stretched out from its mouth with a bullet in its chest and it wasn't moving.

"You killed my best friend," cried Jared as he rubbed its belly and began to ball.

"It's a pest! I did you and the neighborhood a favor. I got to make a phone call to get my wires replaced. Now get that God damn, rabies infested, pest off my lawn!"

Jared went back home to retrieve a wagon, pulled the rat onto it and pulled the wagon home. He buried Zander in the back yard and after he was finished he wrote a eulogy for Zander. He cried when he said it out loud and knew Zander was in rat heaven and he was ok.

Jared rejoiced after grieving an entire month by going to the pet store and brought home another pet rat that was the size of a hamster. He named him Zander the second and rubbed the rat's belly. Jared hoped that it would grow to be as big as his first pet rat, learn tricks and would love getting its belly rubbed.

Fire Starter II: Kill Them All

It was a perfect day in the grade school of Ever Grove Elementary School where the kids attended to learn how they could serve authorities. Gary August sat in his truck and stared at the old school for a long time. There was so many bad times that it became inescapable and Gary wanted to kill them all.

It was a beautiful beginning while it lasted until other students, the cool kids, destroyed it. Why couldn't he have been one of the cool, popular, kids that came to school to be loved by everyone? That was only a fantasy; a fantasy that would end in fire.

Gary got out of his old truck, walked to the back of the tailgate and unraveled the brown tarp. He looked at the flame thrower and machine gun. The Fire Starter took it out and the propane tank that was in the form of a backpack and fastened it to his back. He loved fires because they did such a good job at getting rid of the evidence.

Gary placed a metal helmet that had a visor over his face and a bullet proof vest. The twisted Fire Starter turned around as cars passed by and walked towards the school with the flame thrower and machine gun. He turned on his flame thrower and opened the doors.

He walked past a couple of fourth graders and paid no attention to them. He was only planning to spend ten minutes in his fire rampage to kill all the teachers that did him wrong.

Mrs. Warren, the kindergarten teacher, was in her room with the students when Gary walked in. He engaged the flame thrower and aimed for her head so the children wouldn't catch on fire.

"Mrs. Warren?" he asked.

The kindergarten teacher looked at her former student with fear, but didn't recognize him right away. Then she began to tremble with more fear as she saw the flame thrower. The teacher saw a sneer emerge on his face and recognized it when he drew pictures of people getting shot with his crayons.

"You remember me? You were responsible for holding me back a year. You also took away my toy shark and made me feel bad because I didn't have the same religion as you or the other kids so you can burn in Hell!" shouted Gary.

Before Mrs. Warren could say a word Gary pulled the trigger and watched her face engulf with flames. She screamed hysterically and ran around the room like a chicken with its head cut off. Then she ran into the chalk board, dropped to the floor before going into a seizure and died.

The smell of burnt blood made its way all over the room as the children screamed and ran away. Gary looked at all the children who were scared of him and turned around to leave.

"Hey, you killed my favorite teacher, you murderer!" exclaimed a little girl.

Gary turned around, "I gave your teacher a permanent vacation, do you want a permanent vacation?" he yelled.

"No," she squeaked and cried with her hands up.

"Does anybody else have anything say to me!" The children closed their eyes and began crying as they huddled together. Gary lowered his gun and left the classroom.

The outsider turned on his CD player and put in his favorite song, *Rabies In My Mouth*. He walked down the halls with his flame thrower and torched everyone he remembered as a child that abused him. He kicked in a glass door and started the office staff on fire because they belittled him as a child. He disarmed all the communications of the school and shot his machine gun to make sure the authorities wouldn't be called. Gary walked into the nurses' office and squeezed the trigger for the flame thrower to start the school nurse on fire.

"That's what you deserve," he replied as he heard her crying and rolling around along the floor screaming in pain.

Her skin began peeling off and Gary took off his helmet and headset to watch the nurses' skull emerge as the fire continued to burn.

Gary turned around when he heard a noise and gripped the flame thrower tightly, expecting anything. As soon as he turned the corner of the doorway he was wrestled with by the physical education teacher Mr. Heidel for the flame thrower. Gary quickly kicked him in the balls and hit him in the face with the machine gun. He squeeze the trigger of the flame thrower and scorched the man into a huge blaze of fire.

"Hah! That's for making me run those laps when the cool kids were picking on me in gym class and making me look like a complete loser!"

Mr. Heidel was screaming in pain and screamed in agony, "I was only doing my job!"

The Fire Starter watched Mr. Heidel have a seizure and die. Gary could still hear the gym teacher's voice telling him to ignore the jocks who were teasing him; *just ignore them Gary, they don't know any better*. He could still see their faces like a black and white movie and Mr. Heidel taking the jocks side in an argument. It was the cool kids who had rich parents that paid the teachers salary's that stacked the deck against Gary.

"Your fired," replied the Fire Starter and placed his head set back on and changed the CD to a song called *Johnny Killed The Teacher*.

Gary slid the helmet back on his head with the visor over his eyes and continued his onslaught. He started with the fifth and sixth grade room and shot and killed Mrs. Robbins for dumping his desk multiple times for supposedly not being clean enough. She always gave him a hard time about not having a sharp enough pencil or not being in class on time.

She would always say, "you know you can't be late for work or else you won't have a job."

Gary didn't care because he wanted to be a hired hit man. Mrs. Robbins was in the middle of a spelling-B when Gary walked in. The students were shocked and shakened up to see the serial killer eliminate their teacher with the pull of the trigger.

They didn't know what Gary had to go through in his destroyed mental and emotional past to be where he is now. He turned around and left the room, leaving the students alive.

Gary felt his heartbeat move quickly and tears emerge in his eyes and he lifted the visor to wipe his eyes. The question haunted him; why couldn't he have had a different past? Why couldn't he have gone to a different school to have a life where learning was fun? Why couldn't he live the fairy tales of a student bringing an apple to a teacher? Or even stories when a student actually had crushes on a teacher and think that the teacher was great or lived up to the expectation of a mentor? He would've loved to have brought an apple to school for his favorite teacher that treated him well.

Gary shook these thoughts and realized he had to continue the onslaught. The Fire Starter slid the visor back over his eyes and walked down the hallway to find Mrs. Winters.

Memories filled such mind of abuse of why he couldn't understand a particular math assignment. Mrs. Winters embarrassed him in front of the class and made him feel useless.

"Why can't you get this like the other kids?"

"A third grader could get this why aren't you getting this?"

Gary could hear her nerve racking voice execute his self-esteem, which was like a firing squad. He could feel her hand gripping his neck whenever he was off task. At the time he didn't think about how abusive it was until he got older. Having low self-esteem made him mean and even meaner as the years progressed to everyone. A person with low self-esteem doesn't care about himself or other people's feelings or life.

"Oh my God what is this?" exclaimed Mrs. Winters as her mouth dropped. Gary did the honor of opening up his helmet to reveal himself before lighting the teacher on fire. He slid the helmet back over his head while feeling a lot of satisfaction for pulling the trigger. A huge release was acknowledged from the bad memories and imagined them disintegrating from the fire. Mrs. Winters didn't even get a chance to know what hit her.

"That's for treating me like a piece of crap, embarrassing me in front of the other kids about my intelligents and also giving me detentions for running to the gas station to grab some crème pies!"

After the teacher shook in convulsions while screaming hysterically, she stopped moving and died. Gary raised his helmet and changed his song to *Driving Nails Down Your Spine*. The twisted Fire Starter lowered it back down and walked to the sixth grade room. Gary kicked the door down to see it was Mr. Lexington who stared at him and all the children watched the serial killer point a machine gun at them. The teacher was scared and hid behind the desk, hoping that he wouldn't get killed.

"Hi Mr. Lexington, I decided to pay you a visit and apply the knowledge you taught me in class!" exclaimed Gary as he raised his visor and glared at his old teacher who ridiculed his work.

Mr. Lexington had embarrassed Gary in front of the other students and fill him with doubts. *Why can't you be the smartest kid in the class?* is what Gary would always hear. *You're never going to pass my class if you can't solve this problem. Who do you think you are? Somebody special that we should abide by?* Is what Mr. Lexington would always say.

Mr. Lexington looked at his former student, "do you know how many minutes it takes for the human body to burn?" asked the Fire Starter as he stared at Mr. Lexington who shook his head, scared.

"Well," began Gary. "That's where I need your help, you see you're the one who had me and my classmates dissect those frogs to see how long they can live with an exacto knife opening them up so now I'm going to see how long you can live on fire!"

"Please," began Mr. Lexington as he stuttered, "please don't hurt me."

"Oh I won't kill you I'm just going to start you on fire to see where my experiment goes," said Gary as he pulled the trigger.

Mr. Lexington started screaming as his whole body was consumed by fire. All the kids started screaming as Gary watched Mr. Lexington's body lie still and smelled the stench of burnt blood in the classroom.

The Fire Starter left the room and walked downstairs to see if there was anyone he missed. He walked in the cafeteria and saw the cooks in there and decided to shoot them with his machine gun. They were still alive so he pointed his flame thrower at them and fired. Their bodies lit up like a bonfire and they were dead.

He forgot all about Mrs. Keshal and Mr. Pippin. They were responsible for the teasing and the name calling in school. Gary walked up to the door and changed songs to *I Would Kill You Too (If You Bless Me Too)*.

Gary looked through the little window of the door to see how peaceful the kids were. He saw two teachers sitting in their desk, happy to control the kids' lives.

They were teaching them to turn their parents in to social services if they were ever disciplined for saying no or throwing a temper tantrum. Gary could recognize it and knew it was wrong for any teacher to be sticking their nose into the lives of a family.

The twisted Fire Starter revealed an angry look as he kicked the door in and walked inside. He remembered when the same teacher abused and brain washed him to believe that it was his duty to turn his parents in or anybody's parents for spanking, yelling or aggressively grabbing a child for mouthing off. Gary August was the end product of how society screwed him up and now he was a serial killer. He was a serial killer getting revenge with stupid controlling people.

"Oh my God!" exclaimed Mrs. Mini as she rose out of her seat.

"Hey, you controlling ho! Now is your time to die!" exclaimed Gary.

"Why are you doing this?" she cried as tears welled in her eyes.

"You ruined my life in grade school, junior high and high school. Now I'm getting revenge!"

Suddenly, Mr. Pippin tackled Gary to the floor as the machine gun went off and bullet hit one of the kids. Gary punched Mr. Pippin in the face and got him off of him.

He shot the teacher in the shoulder; kicked him in the face and watched him collapse to the ground. Gary laughed and started him on fire with the flame thrower.

The teacher screamed and cried in pain as he got up in a hurry, but because the fire engulfed his face he couldn't see where he was going and kept hitting the walls before dropping over dead.

Gary turned around to Mrs. Mini and was now aware that his helmet was off and lying on the floor from the struggle with Mr. Pippin. He could hear the chorus coming from his headset. Only the chorus of the last song surfaced to a delightful end of his rampage. The music was in his head feeding his hate like a paper feeds fire.

"Gary August you shot and killed a student and murdered a teacher!"

"Well then, I guess one more teacher isn't going to hurt!" exclaimed Gary as he aimed the flame thrower to her feet and watched her scream in misery as he shot a stream of fire. The fire climbed quickly to her waist, chest, face and she ran like the others. Like a chicken with its head cut off and screamed. Gary hit her in the face with his gun and watched her face burn off when she collapsed to the floor.

"How do you like that bitch! That's for being abusive to me in second grade, when all I wanted was to go home and play with my toys," yelled Gary as he put his helmet back on with the same song on repeat in his head.

Gary left the room and was ambushed by cops, "freeze! Put down your weapons!" yelled the police.

The twisted Fire Starter retreated back into the room while discharging the bullets from his machine gun and killed the cops. More cops showed up and he shot his flame thrower at them to watch them burn.

He left the school and set his weapons, helmet and broken head set back into the box of his truck. He pulled the tarp over them and realized something very strange. The voice in his head was singing his favorite song "Now It's Time". Gary couldn't remember if he left the radio on and realized he was dreaming.

Gary woke up and had been sleeping in his truck. He turned his head to the school before him and was thinking about the dark days. The research indicated all the teachers were still there since the five years he graduated, but it was a school shut down and the students were left home.

The tears filled his eyes and he wiped them as he heard the jokes of who he was. The kid's laughter for picking on him for the way he dressed or the way he looked. Gary dried his eyes and turned the key to the truck, to peel out.

The song "Now It's Time" was playing in his radio and as he drove down the street he reached to his passenger seat and pulled out the detonator for the bombs that he placed inside the school a few weeks ago when he worked as a janitor temporarily. He pushed the button as he chuckled with an evil laugh and heard a big boom from behind him while he drove away.

The school exploded and debris blew a quarter of a mile in circumference. Gary had planted C-4 bombs around the school, enough to blow the school to kingdom come. His next plan was to hunt down the people that picked on him in school. It would take time to locate them, but he would find them and get his revenge. Then he would start looking for people that caused his misery in the first place. Now that his pain was somewhat over he could rest easier knowing that he would kill them all.

Carry's Decision; I Would Have To Be None.

I sit here in this rusted up gas station called Country Boy with the thought in despair of moving forward with my life. The happiest days of my life were the first six months of being treated like an angel by my boyfriend. Even though I feel I'm beautiful I still begin to question myself with these thoughts of doubt of how we would make it in this economic crisis. I think I should answer to my boyfriend's proposal to marry him and make my mother happy. My sister Hannah who is twenty one, thinks I should get married like her.

The phone rings and I answer to give directions or messages to Vic while cashing customers out. One customer I find interesting is the Sunkist guy; he comes in everyday to pay gas and buy bottles of Sunkist. He's so different than the other guys I've met, could it be the angels led him my way? He's so gorgeous; the sound of his voice just makes me light as a feather.

I hear the phone ring again and it annoys me just like my manager does with the record keeping. I'm bored and stare out in space at the shelves filled with potato chips, candy, pop and the freezer full of ice cream. I think how much better I would organize the store while cashing customers out. After the last customer left I pick up the phone to answer.

"Country Boy, how can I help you?"
"Is this Carry?" said the voice, which was a guy.
"Yes, who am I speaking too?" I ask.
"I think you're cute, would you like to go out on a date?"
"I don't date customers and I don't think my boyfriend would like that," I answer as I look at the clock, which was six and rolled my eyes.
"Well you don't have to tell him. We could sneak over to your house which is behind the gas station and do some hanky panky."
"Ok, you're creepy. Don't call back here again, stalker!" I slam the phone on the hook and take a breath. Now would be a good time to call the cops, but then again it could be a prank to get me all wound up. My manager Vic walked out of the room and looked around to see there were no customers.

"Who was that?" he asked.

"A creepy guy," I reply.

"You want to call the cops to escort you home when you're finished with your shift?" he asked

"I don't know yet, probably not because I live so close."

Then my mood changed when the Sunkist guy came back in I felt happy to see a familiar face. I think he's cute, but try not to give him the impression that I'm attracted to him. Even though I think he's hotter than my boy friend. Yes, I could definitely see myself marrying a man like him. I put my hair down and run my fingers through it so he notices me. I'm just interested to see what he does.

"Hi" he said.

"Got fuel?" I ask.

"No just the Sunkist," he replies as I ring it up and he leaves. I don't pay attention to where he's going, but just know that he's leaving. I must be stupid to think that my little fantasy was going to play out.

I bury my thoughts into work and begin sweeping the floor, wiping down counters and cleaning the windows. There are no customers so I put up more hot dogs on the little oven and refill the condiment stand. Before I know it the clock strikes seven o'clock and I punch out to go home.

I walk outside to see it's still daylight and I forget about the creepy guy who called earlier because those things usually happen in the cities. I walk past the corner of the store and suddenly someone grabs me.

I sense it's the creepy guy because he's very strong and is holding a leather glove over my mouth. I resist by biting and hitting, but I get struck down and then knocked unconscious from the sound of a bottle that breaks.

My eyes open and I see it's a man and he's taking his pants off. I look around to see I'm in the woods and have a bad head ache. I touch the top of my head and feel a deep gash in my scalp, my red hair is soaked in blood.

"No, please don't do this," I beg as I try to escape, but I get restrained and feel him grab my ass and rip my underwear off. I pray to God and beg Him to help me.

I turn my head to look at my attacker; I suddenly see someone behind the creepy guy and he attacks him. The angel in flesh beats up my attacker and I faint from the shock.

I wake up after having an amazing dream of flying and realize my hero is the Sunkist guy. I can't believe it and give him a hug as he helps me and hands me my coat and jeans.

"Everything is ok," he says.

"Who are you and where did you come from?" I ask as I get dressed and notice he is turning away to give me privacy to change.

"My name is Michael and you should call the police," he says.

"Will you help me get back?" I ask.

Michael nods and guides me out of the woods and near the trailer court where I see Country Boy. I walk inside and my manager Vic gives me an expression of shock.

"Oh God, what happened to you?"

"I need you to call the police, I was ambushed and Michael saved me."

"Who?" asks Vic.

"Michael," I said as I turn around and Michael is gone. I watch Vic phone the police and walk outside to look for Michael. My mouth drops as I realize that he really was an angel and I would have to be none.

Send In The Clowns

"Price David Williams!" scolded his mother, Dorothy, as she looked at the broken chandelier lamp. She grabbed the boy by the arm and put him in his room.

"You stay in here and think about what you did," his mother yelled as she waved her fingers at the six year old boy who began crying and screaming.

"I don't want be in here," he cried.

"Too bad!" she yelled and slammed the door.

Price started screaming and banged on the door only to hear the sound of the door knob lock. When that didn't do anything he picked up his wooden toys and threw it at the door. He threw himself on the floor and began kicking the door as hard as he could, but the door remained shut.

After thirty minutes of kicking the door, Price walked over to his toy box and opened the lid to play with his puppets, porcelain clown dolls and wooden carriages. Suddenly, the closet door opened and a couple of clowns entered his room.

Price turned his head after hearing the door open and saw the two clowns. At first he was scared, but could see they looked silly and smiled at them.

They were the same size as him with red, white and blue make up on their face with black hair. One was dressed in a red clown suit while the other was dressed in blue and they both had fluffy buttons.

"Hi Price," they said together, "want to play?"

149

"Yes," he said and they introduced themselves as Boy and Girl.

The clown dressed in red was Girl while the one in blue was Boy and they liked Price. They both walked up to Price as though they were going to hug him.

"He is Boy and I'm Girl; we like to party and we should make him into a clown," said Girl.

"Nay he looks fine the way he is!" chuckled Boy.

Boy and Girl finally got down to business and turned around to the closet and clapped their hands to call all the other clowns into the room. Price heard animal sounds and voices coming from his closet.

"It's ok the coast is clear! Let's have a party!" declared Boy.

After turning his head to the closet door, more clowns walked in with different designs of colors and painted faces. Some were skinny and fat while others wore different colors of clothing than Boy and Girl. Hastily, they all came out with musical instruments like trumpets, banjos, violins, pianos and began playing, singing and creating a lot of racket.

Price started laughing and thought it was funny when they came to the chorus of their music. They would squeeze their red nose if they had one to let out the sound of a horn. The clowns began marching on his bed and on the floor near the door pushing the piano.

"More, more!" laughed Price as he clapped his hands.

Then clowns on an elephant entered his room from the closet; they began marching with the clowns that were playing music and doing tricks with weird gadgets. Boy and Girl grabbed Price's hands to sing and dance around his room with the circus music. Then about a dozen little clowns dressed in clown suits stood on Price's bed and began singing as a choir as one clown with a stick directed them to vocalize many different pitches of singing so their voices would glide.

Suddenly, there was a knock at the door and the clowns ran to the closet. Boy and Girl hid under the bed, leaving Price in the middle of his bedroom watching the door unlock and open.

Dorothy, his mother, entered the bedroom and saw everything was a mess, "I heard music and singing in here. Who's in here with you?"

"Clowns," he began. "The clowns Boy and Girl are my friends. They want to sing, dance and party."

"Uh huh," said Dorothy suspiciously as she walked around and then looked at the closet door to hear voices behind it. She walked to the closet door; opened it, turned on the light to see it was full of toys with clothes hung and a shelving unit full of board games. Dorothy scratched her head, turned the light off and walked out before closing the door.

"I want you to clean your room, daddy's coming home and I want you ready for supper."

"Can Boy and Girl help me clean my room?"

"I don't care," she said and left.

After the door was closed, the party started back up again. Boy and Girl slid out from under the bed and began the same routine as before. The marching band, elephant and choir came out of the closet. Boy climbed aboard the elephant to screw a trapeze on the ceiling and began swinging from one end of the bedroom to the next. Price was having so much fun, but he remembered what his mother ordered him to do.

"I have to clean my room!" exclaimed Price.

"Clean your room?" said one clown.

"Yes, clean my room," repeated Girl with the same voice as Price.

Price looked at her bewildered, "how did you do that? You sound like me. How did you do that?"

"It was easy," began Boy using Price's voice to make him laugh, but it only made him mad.

"Stop copying me!" yelled Price.

Swiftly, all the clowns started repeating everything Price said in a song and dance from the last few minutes. Price rubbed his eyes from yelling at the clowns to help him clean up the room. Minutes went by and the room was spotless, but Price was sleeping in his bed.

The door unlocked and the clowns made haste to get to the closet and hide. It was his mother and she had a plate of grilled cheese sandwiches with chicken noodle soup.

"Price wake up," she said and watched her son wake up.

"Mommy I'm sorry I broke the lamp," he said.

"Its ok," she answered and put the food on his dresser to give him a hug.

"You did a good job cleaning your room."

Price opened his eyes wide while giving his mom a hug to see Boy and Girl. The two clowns poked their heads out of the closet door smiling and with a wink they ducked back inside. Price smiled, closed his eyes and continued to hug his mom.

And Then After That

In a town called Deermont, lived a fat, bald man named Bee Dee. He was a man who loved keeping his sanity and enjoyed the simple pleasures of life such as fishing, being single with no children and nobody telling him what to do. The good queen Avah Epona let the people live their life.

One day Bee Dee received a letter from his sister Dee Dee, she needed him to baby sit Hannah for a few hours or more while she left for a job interview. Bee Dee was excited to baby sit his niece Hannah who he hadn't seen for a year.

The uncle pulled up to the cottage in the town of Lana located in the Crescent Kingdom. He got out of his carriage and looked at the little carriage that was owned by his sister and the four donkeys that were tied to a post near the house. He walked up to the door, knocked and right away the door opened and it was Hannah.

Hannah was a typical seven year old girl who had sandy brown hair, blue eyes and an annoying squeaking voice. She hadn't seen her uncle for a while and was excited that he came.

"Hi Uncle," she said.

"Hi, is your mother here?" he asked as he heard Dee Dee's voice.

"Hannah who is it?"

"Mommy, it's Uncle Bee Dee. Can I let him in?"

"Yes dear," said her mother.

Bee Dee stepped into the house and saw his sister Dee Dee walk into the entry. She was dressed in fancy clothes and he could barely recognize her.

"Thanks for making it out here, I've got an appointment with the doctor after the interview," said Dee Dee as she walked to the door.

"Is there anything I need to know?" asked Bee Dee.

"No, I'll be back in a few hours."

"Can we play games?" asked Hannah as she looked up at Bee Dee who looked at his niece with a smile and then at his sister who was smiling.

"I'll be back," said Dee Dee.

"Mommy, mommy where are you going?" asked Hannah.

"Mommy's got to go bye bye."

"But don't you want to stay and play with me?"

"Ask your Uncle Bee Dee, I'm sure he would love to sit and play games with you," answered Dee Dee.

"Oh can ya can ya can ya please?" she asked.

"Ok, fine what would you like to play?" he asked as he watched his sister leave.

"Let's play hide and seek," said Hannah as she watched Bee Dee nod his head, close his eyes and began counting, "ready or not here I come!"

He looked around the living room, checked behind the couch. Searched the kitchen and couldn't find her. Bee Dee walked into her bedroom then looked in the closet full of clothes and still there was nothing. He looked at her bed and then it dawned on him to search under it. He walked up to it; got on his fat knees, peeked his head underneath and heard a scream.

"You found me!" Hannah screamed as she crawled out. "Now it's your turn to hide."

"No that's all right. I'm a fat man that won't be able to hide.

"You're so fat uncle Bee Dee. Why don't you lose weight and then after that you can play hide and seek with me."

"Because I don't want to," he answered.

"But why?" she asked with her annoying squeaky voice.

"Because it's too much work," he answered.

"But why," she asked.

"Because I would have to give up all my sweets," he answered.

"But why?" she repeated.

"It just is," he answered.

"Mommy said that eating to much sweets give you a mouthfull of rotten teeth and a head ache. You know, after I grow up I want to be a dentist. I want to help people with rotten teeth and pull them out. After that, I want to find a man to have babies with and have a daughter that's just like me and call her Danna. Do you think mommy would like that?"

"I have no idea what your mother would think, but don't you want to have fun in your early years before thinking of a man?" asked Bee Dee getting annoyed.

"Mommy said that's when all the fun ends and you look forward to a life of misery. After I find the right man and have my daughter I want to live in a cottage with a rock garden in the front, but I think it would be cool if the house was made out of chocolate. I hope my husband has a lot of money to give me all things I want. And then after that I'll be happy I'll have another baby and call him Danny. And then after that I'll start a new profession as a painter and then while I'm pulling teeth I'll draw my patients facial expression after they've had their teeth pulled and then I'll get paid. What do you think?"

After fifteen minutes Bee Dee couldn't handle it. He tied his niece up to a chair with some rope and tied a stick in her mouth so she couldn't talk. Bee Dee heard her mumble, but it was so incoherent that he just ignored her. After the day ended, he continued to read his book on his sister's couch when Dee Dee got home. She looked the same as before and Bee Dee was happy to see her.

"So how was everything?" she asked.

"Nice and quiet," he smiled.

"Really, how did you do that? I've been trying to get her to shut up without losing my mind."

Bee Dee smiled, "I don't know she just shut up."

Then Dee Dee looked in the living room and saw Hannah tied to a chair with a stick tied in her mouth. Bee Dee smiled and walked out of the house, "I've got to go on a vacation."

"Why did you tie up my daughter?" asked Dee Dee.

"Because she wouldn't shut up," he replied.

"She's just a little girl," answered Dee Dee.

"Beat some manners into her or have some fool watch her," said Bee Dee as he left to go back to his quiet home in Shellmont.

The Jackass

Prince Jack rose up from the naked girl, Evana, whom he had sex with for hours to fulfill his sexual urge and restore his human form. She was beautiful but foolish to get involved with the cursed prince in the first place. Evana looked at Jack strangely and wondered why he was looking at her as though she was the old sea hag.

"Jack, come back to bed and make love to me," she said while cuddled under the covers.

Jack walked back to bed, but stopped to watch her face change to the head of a donkey. Quickly he got dressed to leave as she closed her eyes and was waiting for him. He would be able to continue without worrying about his own changes from the curse of the warlock, Jem.

"Why are you getting dressed in such a big hurry?" she asked as ears of a donkey began to appear and her face became hairy. Suddenly, she noticed her nose was larger and connected with her mouth.

"What's happening to me!" she exclaimed as she jumped out of bed and ran to a mirror. "Oh my God, I'm a donkey!" she screamed as Jack slipped out the door before she knew he was gone.

Prince Jack felt relieved that he was able to keep his human form this time and for this long. Other times he had to kidnap women and rape them in order to maintain his human form. For months, he had lived with this curse of having the head of a donkey if he didn't seduce young women for sex.

He remembered when he was prince of Lustra Kingdom and ruled it with his older brother Prince Randar. Until he met the warlock who said that he would have the ability to make people laugh without a word and that he would quickly learn how to seduce women to be handsome.

The warlock told Jack, after realizing he made a mistake of agreeing to the terms, that the spell would be broken after he found a woman with the same curse and become the most amazing family that the world had ever seen.

Prince Jack scratched his head to the thought of being the villain and an ass. He realized that being the hero would never happen and he would have to seduce women for the rest of his life.

Prince Jack walked the streets of Destiny Port, forgetting about Evana and moved on to the next woman that would inherit his curse. In his mind, he could still hear the screaming from Evana, who was left in the house as a jackass. He remembered how he ran away like a jack rabbit so she wouldn't catch him. Not that there was anything Evana could do except sound like a donkey. The girl was a complete whore anyways and deserved it.

The rest of the day Jack lied under a tree and stared at the clouds. He dreamed about the life that men his age were doing. Working a job and then coming home to make love to their wives. He wished that he could have that life, but realized that it was hopeless to dream, his future was to be a jackass.

Sooner or later, he would not get so lucky and he would be changed into a complete jackass. He would become a donkey and a slave master would buy him. Jack would end up slaving away, hauling a carriage for a peddler or a young couple. Then he would be forced to breed with some female donkey that he didn't know and she would give birth to a little jackass. All these thoughts were disturbing and Jack tried to think of something else that was pleasant.

Jack looked at himself in the water of Crystal Lake. He was feeling sad, empty and wondered if the great Queen, Avah Epona, of Shellmont could help him break the spell. No she would not because the queen was a seer that would tell him his purpose was to be a jackass, use women for sex, breed whores and little, bastard, jackasses.

Accepting his new life would be difficult and Jack would have to accept it. The prince looked around and realized that there was an abundance of small apple trees. He could stay here for days until he decided what to do next. Maybe he would wake up from this nightmare.

Four days passed and Jack fulfilled the time by eating apples, bathing in the lake and soaking up the sun. With all the emotional pain bestowed him upon from the past, he had to feel some good in his life. Except every night, while he was asleep he would have nightmares of Jem laughing at him as a donkey pulling his carriage.

It was morning and Jack turned his head to the rising sun and opened his eyes to see a woman emerge from the water. The girl looked like she was sixteen years old; had long black hair with aqua blue eyes and she was naked coming out of the water. At first Jack thought she was a mermaid. Then he realized that she was human and beautiful with the sun hitting her body from behind.

"I'm sorry I thought these lands were uninhabited," said the girl.

"That's all right, you can do whatever you want," said Jack as he got up.

The girl was quiet and looked at him strangely, "you don't think it's strange seeing me this way?"

"Not at all," he began with a smile.

"I think I should go," she answered.

"No wait, I want you to stay!" he said.

The girl looked at him surprised and even though she was naked she decided to stay to get to know him. The prince watched her shiver from having the wet hair and gave her his cotton coat.

"My name is Sophie."

"I'm Prince Jack."

"Prince huh," she smiled.

"Why are you naked?" asked Jack.

"I'm being naughty," she smiled and looked at Jack who smiled back, thinking he had a new victim to keep him from changing. "My father is Jed; he's a farmer and as a family we have strict rules. I decided to get away and break all the rules."

"So you decided to swim in a lake naked?"

"There's no harm in skinny dipping as long as nobody knows about it. You won't tell my parents will you?" she asked.

"No, not unless you give me something," replied Jack.

"What do you want?" she asked suspiciously.

"I want you," he replied and then watched the girls face squirm in a disgusting look.

"I'm a virgin and wish to wait until I get married."

"But they'll never know and it's great to lose your virginity," persuaded Jack.

Sophie looked at him puzzled, "no that's ok I'll wait until I'm married. I want to be surprised and besides I think my mother would be disappointed to learn I was whoring behind her back."

"They'll never know," he continued.

"What kingdom do you rule?" she asked to change the subject.

Then suddenly Jack's face became hairy and ears of a donkey emerged from his head. She laughed at him and Jack realized he was changing.

"You have to help me," begged Jack as he grabbed her ankles and got on top of her.

"No! Get off of me you jackass," Sophie screamed as she slapped, kicked and punched the prince. She ran into the lake and was in two feet of water until she was tackled by the prince again. Except this time he had removed his pants and was having an erection.

Sophie screamed in terror and started crying as she felt the prince trying to separate her legs to get inside her. She saw a stick floating nearby and grabbed it with her hand but before he could penatrate her, Sophie hit him in the face as hard as she could. Jack screamed in pain and covered his face then she hit him in the crotch with the stick to ensure her escape. Jack let out another sound like a donkey as he watched her swim in deeper water.

"I'll tell your parents and everybody in the area you had sex with me and then you'll be labeled a whore!" he yelled.

"Go ahead! Everyone will laugh at you and call you a jackass!"

Jack said nothing and watched her swim away in the distance until she was gone. Then he began to well up with tears and felt like an ass. No woman would be fooled to have sex with him if he had the head of a donkey.

Jack got out of the water and felt sore from being struck in the face and the crotch. He would surely need to recover and rethink his plan.

The prince looked around after a few hours of resting and decided to walk back to Destiny Port. There would have to be someone he could rape that would help him change back. An old lady or a naïve teenage girl that would give him what he needed. He found nothing, but a hill with a forest. He walked up the hill to look at the big lake again and was excited to see what looked like the same girl who escaped him earlier.

She was facing the lake and had her head in the water and was squeezing her hair to drain the water. Jack licked his lips and took off his pants and had an erection once again.

"You won't get away this time," he whispered as he ran up and raped her.

For long hours they were stuck together and he was enjoying himself with his eyes closed; he finally stopped and waited for his true form to come back, but it never happened. The girl turned around to reveal that she had the face of a donkey and let out an awkward sound that a donkey lets out as she raised what was suppose to be her hand, but now was a hoof.

"Oh no," he replied as he realized he was changing into a full-fledge donkey.

First his hands turned into hooves and his body became hairy, then furry. His feet turned into hooves and then a tail popped out, above his ass. He tried to cry for help, but only let out a, "he-honk!"

A man came out from behind the hill. He was handsome and looked like a magician because he wore a black robe. On the robe were gold threads of the moon and the sun. Before both donkeys could escape, he lassoed and pulled them to the wagon. He took off the big hood to reveal his long blonde hair and dark brown eyes. Both donkeys looked at the warlock in fear and tried to scramble, but the man gripped the rope tightly.

"I promised you, you would be able to make the world laugh without a word, but I need you both to form the most amazing family that everyone will ever see, a family of jackasses!" he laughed.

Years passed and Prince Jack had a family with the female donkey, named Edna. They traveled to Shellmont where Jack and his whole family were sold to farmer Jed. There was a girl standing next to Jed that looked like Sophie.

"Well Sophia what do you think of the donkeys?"

She looked at Jack who looked sad at the virgin girl that escaped and listened to her talk, "treat them well father, I think they'll work for us quite well."

The farmer looked pleased at the family of donkeys and the warlock cracked a grin. They were sold and became property of the farmer who overworked, beat and whipped them. Prince Jack would keep producing more donkeys for the farmer to be sold. He and Edna would be the spectacle for everyone to laugh at and the grandest family the world had ever seen.

The Flesh Beast III: The Snap of Your Bones

You wake up to hear something outside the door of your room. It was weeks since you remembered the reason why you were in this hell hole. You were protesting against your parents for making you into a slave. You were right and they were wrong. Now that you're in the Insane Asylum for Boys and Girls you might as well make the most of it. You hear children talk about a beast that eats children and you're scared that you're going to be next.

Once again you hear something outside your door and you get out of bed to see what it is. You reach for the door knob with your nine year old hand and open the door. It's Jamie and Charlotte and they look at you with a smile.

"Hey, I heard something down the hallway from our bedrooms," replied Jamie.

"Yeah, it's probably the flesh beast!" yelled Charlotte.

"Shh, you want to wake the dead?"

"Sorry," she answered.

"Quiet, I hear something," said Jamie as he held out his hand.

You become suspicious because you feel like you're being toyed around by your two friends, but you follow them down the hallway. It's dark and you're unable to see what's in front of you. Suddenly, the moon unveils from the clouds and you can see what's in front of you. The moon is full and you're able to hear the wind blow through the evergreens because the windows are open. It seems like all is well and you keep following your friends who are in front of you. Then you stop when they do, after hearing something dreadful.

"Where's my flesh?" it whispers and you look ahead to see a pair of glowing yellow eyes stare at you.

You scream in horror and run back, leaving your two friends behind while they scream. There's no time to turn around to see where it is and you don't care. All you care about is getting yourself out of harm's way, but you hear a thumping behind you. The ripping sound of a growl the scream of one of your two friends echoes throughout the hallway. You turn your head to see what it is and watch it tear the head off of Jamie with a single snap of its jaws. You can see its shiny teeth run up and down its jaw bone and your skin begins to crawl. The blood turns cold as your body starts to curdle and you feel your legs become weak while it charges after Charlotte.   She screams and shouts for you to help her, but your body is numb and you can't move. You close your eyes and cry as you hear the snap of her bones.

You finally get the strength in your heart to run and you hope that it doesn't grab your legs and eat them. Each stride you make, you hear the beast charge after you as it repeats, "where's my flesh!"

You get to the door and can't open it. Then you hear the beast growl at you and you slowly turn around while the tears well up in your eyes. You look at the eight foot beast and watch the teeth run up and down its jaw bone like a chainsaw as it yells "where's my flesh!"

You urinate on the floor because you're so scared and that's when you close your eyes to expect the worst as you unleash a scream. You can already feel your legs getting ripped off from the flesh beast. You can't breathe and you're gasping for air.

All of a sudden, you open your eyes after screaming for a long time. All the children get out of their rooms and into yours to see what is going on. They see you in your pajamas soaked with piss. Your cheeks are covered with sweat and tears and you take deep breaths.

Ms. Knealson walks up to you in her black night gown. She looks disturbed and you momentarily see the pupil of her eyes turn yellow then back to black. The other children start laughing at you because you urinated in you pajamas and woke up Ms. Knealson.

"Get back to your rooms!" she orders with the wave of her finger as the kids close the door and the hag turns to you.

"What seems to be the problem?"

"I saw what's been eating the children," you say as you point to where Jamie and Charlotte's bodies would be, but when you look you see that they're gone. There is no evidence that they were lost.

"I don't know what you're talking about," says Ms. Knealson.

You get scared as you see her pointy teeth, "but I saw it?"

"You saw what your mind wanted you to see," answered Ms. Knealson with a sneer.

"Jamie and Charlotte were eaten alive!" you cry.

"I don't know a Jamie or a Charlotte and you're going to do me services for lying," says Ms. Knealson as she grabs you by the ear and forces you down corridors and staircases to a room full of grandfather clocks.

"Get in there and don't come out until every clock is sparkling clean!" she yells while lighting a candle.

You look around to see numerous amounts of clocks and nearby is a small skeleton with a pale of water. You freak out and scream when you see the skeleton of a child that was presumably cleaning as a slave.

"Adam was a good servant, but he kept missing spots, but now you're replacing him, please do a good job this time!" says Ms. Knealson as she turns away and then you hear the slam of the door.

You look around and you fill up the bucket in a sink with a water pump. You turn around after hearing each clock whisper, *where's my flesh?*

In the glass you can see the image of the flesh beast opening its mouth and you can also see arms creep in and out of the clock. You let out a scream, dropping the candle and realize you're never going home. Then the light goes out and you hear the sound of a wood splitter echo the room. Then a wicked voice yells, "where's my flesh." You feel something grab you before tearing your limbs off and now you're dead.

The Tooth Fairies

Donnie got on the school bus and ran to sit with Michael. It was like any other day and Michael was his buddy. The two six year olds had a lot to talk about. Especially since it was their first day of school and instead of Michael losing his front top and bottom he lost all his teeth.

"How did you lose your teeth Michael?" asked Donnie.

"I got beat up by three goblins with yellow eyes and hooded robes," began Michael.

"Yeah right, you just got lucky and the tooth fairies came to barter you with more money," laughed Donnie.

"I'm telling you the truth."

"How do you know they were goblins?" asked Donnie.

"Because I escaped from them and turned on the lights. I saw their leather green skin and beak like mouths," replied Michael.

Donnie stared at his best friend and all the teeth he was missing. Surely Michael was making it all up to scare him. Then the thought emerged that his own front teeth were wiggly and the goblins would come and take them.

"They took all my teeth and said that they're coming for you."

"They're not going to get in my room. My windows are locked and my mommy locks the doors," declared Donnie.

"They come out from under our beds, from an underworld of goblins that turn teeth into gold nuggets," replied Michael seriously.

How do you know they turn teeth into gold nuggets?"

"They told me."

"Why don't they go after animals or dead bodies from the cemetery?"

"I don't know."

The two kids didn't say anything for the rest of the bus ride. Donnie tried to forget about it at recess, but after he was finished playing soccer the tooth fairies entered his mind. The hours at school came to a close when he arrived home and felt relieved that the day was over.

Donnie walked inside the door and was greeted by his fat mom with ugly red hair that was tied up into a bun. She was sweet, loving and always kissed her son on the cheek, but her breath reeked of onions. The boy wasn't in the mood because he was anxious about losing his teeth.

"Hello honey, how was school today?" she smiled and hugged him.

"Fine, mother is there such thing as a tooth fairy?" he asked.

"Of course sugar pops," began his mother. "Why do you have wiggly teeth that need to be pulled?" she giggled with a snort.

Donnie covered his mouth and then renounced it, "yes I do mommy."

His mother kneeled down and pulled out her hand, "let me wiggle one, dear."

Donnie opened up his mouth and felt his mother wiggle his tooth, "oh it's loose, you know the tooth fairy may come tonight and give you a quarter for it."

"That's what I'm afraid of mommy; Michael said that he was visited by three goblins with yellow eyes that beat him up and took all his teeth."

"No honey he was just saying that to scare you," declared his mother.

"But mom, all his teeth are gone."

"Donald, he probably had them taken out from all the junk food and cotton candy he ate at the fair. Little boys that get spoiled by their parents rot their teeth out and he told you a whole heap of garbage to get you all worked up. No, the tooth fairy isn't going to rip out all your teeth," she chuckled like a pig.

"Wow, thanks for telling me mommy. Now I won't be scared anymore," he replied as he wiped the sweat from his forehead.

Donnie ate supper with his mom and watched a movie that suddenly reminded him of the goblins that Michael described. The little boy began to bite his finger nails and felt the pain in his teeth. His mother walked over to the television and turned it off.

"I want you to get ready for your bath, you've watched enough of this garbage to have nightmares," ordered his mother.

Donnie got ready for his bath and after he was finished, he dressed in his pajamas and was tucked into bed by his mother. His mother went to bed to prepare for tomorrow. Donnie lied in bed with the nightlight on and stared at the ceiling as he waited for sleep to take him.

The night was quiet and the hours seemed long. The ringing in his ears persisted until suddenly he heard something that sounded like a trapdoor and then something crawled out from under his bed. Donnie began biting his fingernails and looked around the room. His mother was in bed and wouldn't be able to save him. All of a sudden, three little creatures wearing raggedy robes with funny little top hats came out from under his bed.

"Is this the right room Boss?" said one of them as he lit a candle while the other two lit theirs.

"Of course this is the right place Right Wing," said another voice.

"I don't know Boss; every time we go into another little boy's bedroom I get confused. I think we're in the wrong one."

"Shut up Left Wing! This is the right place," replied another voice and Donnie looked to see the one in the middle point at him.

Donnie began crying as he saw all three of the goblins approach him. They were about four feet tall and smelled like ice cream, but looked hideous with beak like mouths and yellow glowing eyes. When they lightly touched the blanket where his arm was he could feel their long, sharp, fingernails.

They slowly crawled up on his bed and when they opened their mouth to smile he could see their pointed teeth. He could see their green leathery skin and the glowing yellow eyes. His blood turned into ice as he began to hyperventilate.

"Nice Donnie, good little Donnie, all we want is your teeth," chuckled Right Wing.

"Quickly hold him down while I get the tools," ordered Boss.

Right Wing and Left Wing covered the boy's mouth and held his arms down while Boss pulled out a strange contraption that looked like pliers. Donnie tried to scream for his life, but he couldn't and felt powerless.

"Now this won't hurt a bit," assured Boss as he smiled and began putting a metal device in the boy's mouth to force his mouth to stay open so each tooth could get gripped, one at a time.

He started with the front teeth and blood spurted everywhere. Then they moved towards the back and more blood began flooding the child's mouth while he cried. The little boy felt the metallic taste of blood on his tongue that flowed down his throat.

Donnie continued to cry and did everything to fight back, but Boss got angry and punched Donnie in the face. The goblin continued to pull the other molars on the other side. Right Wing and Left Wing were giggling as Donnie kept screaming and moving his head back and forth.

"Hey Boss, he won't sit still. I think you need to hit him again," laughed Right Wing.

Boss began grunting in anger and punched Donnie in the face again. He was able to get the child to sit still as he pulled the remainder of the teeth. Very quickly, the last tooth was pulled until Donnie was toothless. Boss pulled his metal contraption that held his mouth open.

"Good boy," laughed Boss as he patted him on the cheek then clocked him hard and heard Donnie unleash a wail of a cry that blended with his scream.

Quickly, the goblins ran under the bed and chuckled. Now they had all the teeth that belonged to Donnie to make them into gold.

"One last spoiled brat to worry about," declared Left Wing.

Donnie let out another wail like no other and then his mother cascaded through the door to see blood all over his pillow and blankets. Donnie had a bloody nose and blood streaming down his chin from his mouth.

"What in heavens happened child?"

"The creatures came and took my teeth," cried Donnie.

His mother's mouth dropped opened and couldn't believe all his teeth were gone. She called the police and they did an investigation, but couldn't find any evidence of foul play. She brought Donnie to the Emergency Room and the doctors said he was ok and that his gums would heal. They were astonished that all Donnie's teeth were gone, but there was nothing they could do.

Two days later, in the morning Donnie sat next to Michael on the bus and the two were quiet as they looked at each other petrified. They both knew that the tooth fairies paid them a visit to collect their teeth. Michael leaned over to whisper in Donnie's ear, "I told you they were coming for you."

Believe in Your Dreams

Dedicated to Trent Landry.

I walk around the center of the track field and I feel excitement in the air. It's a sunny day and a breeze hits my face as I hear the announcer direct what races are coming. It's so hard to take all the commotion in, so I take my time and wait my turn to run the four-hundred meter dash.   There are ten different schools competing and it's the last meet of the season. It's very competitive for me and even though I'm a fast runner I keep my ego in check because there is one guy who can run faster than me and his name is Trip Roads

I look at my watch and it's time for me to do my long jump. I watch all the long jumpers line up ready to run and make the longest jump that can be accomplished. It's my turn and I'm nervous because of the fear of failing.

I take a deep breath and begin running. My legs move up and down with each push from my toes. I can see the white line and I prepare my jump. I let go and swing my legs out and fly like a bird before landing in the sand. My distance is measured and it's sixteen feet. I try two more times and it's a little easier to do without feeling nervous. I don't score as well and decide to make a move at the track after hearing the four-hundred meter dash being called.

All the guys running in the race brag about how fast they can run. Everyone looks athletic, confident and I question if I should even be in this race. There are four guys from Somerset and the man in charge decides to break us up into two heats. I look around for Trip Roads and then I see him standing next to the man in charge. The referee looks at me and Trip just as I feel ice fill my veins.

"You two are going in the faster heat after they are done," said the referee.

I get anxious and begin to think I'm not fast enough. I turn to look at Trip; he's looking at me and slowly he smiles with confidence. I take a deep breath and try to relax, my hands are sweaty and I get like that when I'm anxious. I see our runners up ahead behind the starting line and their staggered on the track. I watch them kneel down and get in position. The gun fires and they begin running. My heart's pumping faster and I feel exhilarated watching them run as well as the hope for one of them from my school to place first.

I turn my head to Trip and he's wearing a black wind breaker jacket that says Somerset Track on the back and his hands are in his pockets. He says nothing to our opponents, who are talking to each other.

"Aren't you nervous?" I ask him.

Trip looks at me with his brown eyes and a gust wind brushes through his hair, "why?"

"How fast can you run it?"

"About a minute and three seconds," I answer.

"Why don't you run it under a minute?"

"Because I can't," I reply.

"You'll never know unless you try."

I begin to smile at Trip and feel very inspired to run with him. He doesn't care what other people think and doesn't worry because he never loses. I think Trip is amazing and I hear a voice in my own head telling me that I could be like him. I could run like him and become a winner just like him. There is a problem, I know I could never be inspiring like Trip Roads, the fastest kid in junior high.

We hear the referee call everyone over and we're designated to eight lanes of the track. I'm in the fifth lane and Trip is in the first one. I feel an adrenaline rush stretch from my neck and shoulders to my legs. The sun is overhead and the wind runs through my hair as we all walk up to the starting line. I hear the roar of the crowd cheering for us and as I get in position, the hair on the back of my neck stands up. I wait for the gun to fire, which feels like eternity.

The gun fires and immediately I take off from the starting line. I run as fast as I can and take deep breaths while feeling my heart pump harder. I pass the other guys in the right lanes that had a head start. I enter the straight away and feel my lungs burn while I begin thinking of the past.

A flashback from kindergarten entered my mind when I first met Trip and tried to beat him in a race. I suddenly look in the corner of my eye and see Trip running past me in the first lane and the track begins to curve to where the two-hundred meter dash would start. My muscles begin to tire, but I keep running fast. Trip is about ten feet ahead of me and two guys pass me.

One is in the second lane and the other is in the fourth lane. I follow the curve and approached the straight away to the finish line. The crowd goes nuts while cheering really loud and I closed my eyes for a second to keep the tears from falling on my cheeks because the wind is hitting my eyes.

I see Trip way ahead and the two racers were just a little bit ahead of me and as we approached the finish line. I finish in fourth place and my time is fifty-nine seconds. I take deep breaths and placed my hands over the back of my head. I never ran that hard in my life. Then I saw Trip walking around doing the same thing. He walks up to me, "how did you do?"

I tell him as he nods his head with a smile, "I knew you could do it."

I feel a burst of confidence pour inside me that there is nothing I can't do. I feel inspired to take on the world and face any problem. I watch him walk away and forever feel changed into the person I'm meant to be.

An Angel Visit III: Heaven

After cleaning his room Rya sat at his computer and waited for inspiration. When realizing the creativity was reaching his thoughts he put on some Celtic music; lied in bed and began daydreaming about the angel book yet to be written.

Krissy was out of his life and Alyssa moved on. He loved Alyssa and in a flashback remembered the love they shared. He was certain that when the months progressed there would have been more between them.

The writer closed his eyes and his breathing slowed as he felt himself leave his body. He was drifting farther away from the Earth plane and into the heavens. Drifting away like a piece of wood, drifting down a river.

Rya opened his eyes and raised his head see he was in a strange place. A room full of staircases with many rooms high above that he could see into them like a doll house. There was nobody around, except him, and he was confused as to why he was here.

"Hello!" he yelled with an echo, but there was no reply.

The structure around him was remarkable and as he touched the railing, he felt its smooth rock texture. His sense of touch against the surface was confusing because the bricks were rock, but when he pressed down it was like a pillow.

Swiftly, Rya felt a hand touch his shoulder and turned around to see it was an angel. She had long blonde hair, blue eyes and elegant white skin.

"Sarah?" he smiled.
"Yes," she smiled.
"This is your home?" he asked.
"Not exactly," she began. "This is *our* home."
Rya looked around and didn't understand the answer, "our home, but my home is in my apartment in Hustle."
"Yes, but this is where we all go to play and visit. We share this structure with other angels and souls."
"This is where we go when we die," said Rya

Abruptly, there were more angels that walked down the stairs to visit Rya. They were beautiful and wore white robes, gold tunics, armor and crowns. They smiled at Rya as they walked towards him and held out their hands.

"Sarah, who are they and what do they want?"

Suddenly, the angels began shaking his hand, kissing and hugging him. It was difficult to distinguish male from female, but gradually it became easy to determine. Child-like angels grouped around Rya and hugged him as little children do. They began laughing and ran away behind the bigger angels as they came forward.

"They wanted to meet you," answered Sarah with a smile.

Then Rya met an angel with long black hair stretching to her waist. She carried a sword, but it was in

176

its sheath. She looked similar in facial traits to Sarah and Krissy, but her eyes were brown and she looked a little muscular than Sarah. The black haired angel wore a beautiful white gown with a gold belt that held the matching sheath.

"You two look alike," said Rya smiling.
"Yeah, we get that a lot," said the archangel.
"This is Sarrjel," said Sarah as she watched Rya shake the archangel's hand.
"She fought and killed the fallen angels that were in your apartment during your testing period."

The writer looked around to see there were about a hundred angels around him, still shaking his hand and giving him affection. There were angels everywhere and he watched them pull out their harps, trumpets and violins. Rapidly, he noticed a choir forming as they began singing in gregorian chants.

Holy Holy Holy
Holy Holy Holly
make way for our lord

Holy Holy Holy
Holy Holy Holy
make way for our lord
Rya will write every word

Rya looked at them while smiling and didn't know what to think. Clearly they wanted him to write about them and it was inspiring to watch.

"Now if you'll excuse me I must join them," replied Sarah as she left to be in the choir.

Then the music stopped and the angels flew in different directions. They glided down from the air and stood next to Rya as they all witnessed The King of Kings, Jesus.

The angels praised Him with their chants and He was accompanied by two archangels that looked slightly like a young John Kerry with the body of a body builder.

When Jesus looked at Rya, he smiled and held out his hand. He looked like a Jew and was wearing a white robe and had a white glow around him.

Rya took Jesus' hand and they walked up the stairs with the two archangels and began walking while the angels continued to sing with their faces appearing in the brick of the structure. Rya could hear the gregorian chants on the way up and felt the hair on the back of his neck stand up.

"Don't be scared to speak," He said.

"Why am I here?" asked Rya.

"I thought you knew," He replied as the angels stopped chanting and listened. Rya took a deep breath and began thinking about his own life when he was misunderstood.

"I know who you are and the endeavors you've faced. The people are mis-directed. They're hungry for God and seek answers to such questions, that is why I need you."

"To do what?" asked Rya.

"I want you to write for me."

"Write for you, I don't understand? You have priests and the pope to do your writings," said Rya.

"My teachings have become corrupted and taken advantage of. You can write for me and carry my words. You have a hundred angels to protect you from evil so that you'll be safe, isn't that right Archangel Michael and Archangel Raphael," declared Jesus.

Rya's eyes widened and didn't realize who the archangels were until now. Jesus leaned forward, "go and tell others what God has done for you."

Rya watched Him snap his fingers and before he knew it, everything shifted to a blur.

Rya woke up in his room and at first felt dizzy. He felt like he had a telephone call from God and had the desire to do some writing. The writer knew he would never forget about this phenomenon.

Then the troubling thought came to pass, how would he know what was to be written? Then the thought of Sarah entered his mind and he looked at the illustration of her that was hung above his computer monitor and began to laugh.

<u>She Says II</u>: A Visit From Grandma

The afternoon was abnormally beautiful than he thought it was supposed to be. He was on his way to his grandma's house that he visited for a long time, since he was a child. As soon as he stepped in he saw grandpa standing in the kitchen next to the entrance of the living room. He was dressed in his usual white t-shirt and jeans his hair was white, but he looked healthy before he passed away.

"It's about time, where have you been?" asked grandpa as he smiled.

Barber just looked at him shocked and couldn't believe it was him. They stood eye level to each other and smiled as though his grandpa returned from a vacation.

Barber woke up from the dream and realized how weird it was. He remembered his grandpa as stubborn and unhealthy, but the dream revealed he was healthy, happy and alive.

He missed his grandma and didn't know where she was. He only hoped that things were moving along for her in the afterlife.

Morning had come and things were pretty much back to normal except the occasional painful memories that grandma was gone. Caroline had moved on with her life as did May and they were looking for fruitful opportunities to make money with their talents. Barber was still working at One Way Ship Services, but he didn't have to work because it was Saturday.

The day flew by and Barber lost track of the time when he realized it was twenty minutes after ten at night and he wanted to get an early rise tomorrow. He turned off the television; laid in bed to relax and thought about nothing, but all that came up was his grandma. Her face, voice and smile embedded into him like a nail driven into a piece of wood.

Barber woke up and found himself on the beach. He could hear the waves of water splash on shore and wondered where he was. He wasn't in a place that he recognized, but it seemed familiar to him from the beginning of time. The sun seemed so much brighter and larger. The clouds were filled with pink, purple and orange.

The sand on the beach was white and when he stepped off from the beach to the warm water. It was unlike any beach where the water was cold and gross. For some reason he knew that his grandma was here and decided to look for her. Barber began walking up the sandy lot and began to playfully run and jump over the waves like a kid again.

He stopped to look at his left and saw someone lying down on the beach about twenty feet from him. It was her and she was lying under a palm tree with a large umbrealla wearing her usual clothes when she was alive. His grandma looked healthy, happy, young and at peace. Barber walked up to the woman he knew as his grandma and couldn't believe it was her, but before she opened her eyes she smiled and the dream was over.

Barber woke up in his bed, full of emotion and realized he was dreaming. He knew that the beach was somewhere on the VHS tapes that his father used to record.

The young man got out of bed and walked around the house to find nobody home. The TV was on with the sound of the water washing up to the shore and it made Barber squirm with excitement.

Barber looked at the television to see the waves wash up on the sand and the same sight of beauty that he saw before. The only difference was the film was in black and white. The visuals moved the way he did in his dream and when he came upon the sight of his grandmother lying under the palm tree with the large umbrella over her and he began to laugh. She was under the palm tree wearing the same clothes she wore when she was alive. She looked so peaceful; so happy especially when she revealed a smile and opened her eyes for Barber to see until the tape went static. Suddenly, Barber felt a weight of emotion, a click in his brain that unleashed a euphoria like nothing before. Grandma was ok and that much was certain.

"Grandma's ok!" cried Barber with a smile. "She's doing fine, everything is fine!" he repeated over and over again with a gasp.

Slowly Barber looked around inside the house, thinking he wasn't alone, but nobody was around, but he wanted everyone to know what he learned and continued.

"Everything is ok!" he exclaimed with a smile as his eyes became teary eyed.
"Grandma is alive and wants us to know she's ok!" he yelled as he ran from one room to the next to tell his family, but couldn't find them and then he realized something. He was still dreaming.

Barber woke up from the dream in a dream with a gasp because it caught him by surprise. It was like a telephone call from grandma and he began to cry as he got up because he realized she was ok.

It was morning and he could hear his family talking in the kitchen. He could smell the breakfast from the kitchen into his bedroom, but it was secondary to what was on his mind.

Barber walked out of his room and down the hallway to the kitchen to see everybody eating breakfast and they looked at him.

"Well look who decided to wake up," replied his mom.

"What's going on?" asked his dad.

"Grandma visited me in my dream to let us know she's ok."

Everybody was quiet as Barber explained his dream. Caroline remembered her last words with grandma and took a breath since it was more than she could handle.

"It was amazing," continued Barber.

"I never had a dream like this, it felt so comforting and beautiful. I woke up and thought the dream had ended and when I walked into the living room I saw everything from the dream on the television. I watched it and when I saw her, she smiled and opened her eyes, then the tape went static."

May and Lanett looked at Barber curiously but remained quiet. Then Caroline began crying since she wasn't able to contain herself. Lanet gave her a hug to comfort her.

"Do you think I'm crazy?" asked Barber.
"Maybe she did visit you," replied May.
"So what do we do now?" asked Barber.
"I don't know," said his mother.
"She obviously wanted us to know that everything is ok and everything is ok," declared Barber as he sat down and they talked about their memories with grandma.

The Rototiller Bitch

Dedicated to Sean.

It was near midnight and the little boy Trunt was angry because he was sent to bed early at seven o'clock for being dis-obedient. Trunt wanted to get revenge with his parents and make them pay for sending him to bed early.

Charlotte and Greg were relaxing in the living room; watching adult theater from an oracle. Greg worked long hours at the hardware store and hardly got to see his wife. The days of being together and reflecting on their fine qualities were gone.

The only thing to look forward to was working at his job none stop to pay for the house, property, taxes, and Trunt. Their marriage was taking a backseat and they were losing connection. It was nice to be home and both parents were happy to have some time alone from their son, who was a handful.

It soon grew late and Trunt was playing with his stuffed animals when he heard them walk past the door. A sneer emerged on Trunt's face as he looked at the clock and waited for it to strike midnight. There was nothing to hear accept the ringing in his ears. Suddenly, Trunt let out a loud scream that was unbearable.

Trunt kept screaming as his parents cascaded through the door. Charlotte picked up the little man as his dad tried to wake up while rubbing his eyes. They were both trying to get to sleep because they had to work in the morning. Trunt's father let out a yawn and looked at his son through the candle lit room.

"What's the matter?" she asked.

Trunt couldn't think of what to say and decided to make up one of his fictional characters when playing in his room. He did play games with a creature that had rototiller blades on her head. They played hide and go seek and she was his imaginary friend, or was she? Actually for the reader; the rototiller bitch is a creature from another world that is a different race that uses the name like the boogeyman.

"The rototiller bitch is in my room!"

"Trunt that's not very nice to say to your mother. You know there is no swearing allowed," ordered his father.

"Yeah, I suppose your right," answered Trunt with a smile.

"I'm glad you're here."

They tucked their son in bed and gave him a kiss good night.

"Sleep tight and don't let the boogey man get you," replied Greg as they kissed him goodnight and blew out the candle before closing the door.

Greg kissed his wife when they got into their room and picked her up in his arms while walking to bed. Charlotte smiled as they lied down and she could feel his strong hands touch her abdomen. She reached her hands to touch his bristly face and remembered that it had been a long time since they made love. They were about to take off their clothes when they heard a scream from Trunt's bedroom. They got out of bed once again to see what the problem was. They could hear him screaming none stop like he was on fire.

Greg opened the door and they walked in with a lamp. Charlotte walked over to her son and calmed him down by giving him a hug. Little Trunt looked scared and was clammy.

"What's the matter?" she asked.

"The rototiller bitch came out of by closet!"

"What did we say about swearing?" asked Greg.

"It's not nice to swear in front of mommy, but that's her name," cried Trunt.

"I don't care, I don't want to hear that kind of language coming from you," said Greg. "Now honey, I want you to try to get some sleep," said Charlotte as she kissed him on the cheek and left with Greg.

Greg and Charlotte were back in their bedroom, making love under the covers and embracing each other in oneness like no other. After hours of kissing and touching they heard some more screaming.

"What the hell! We can't be alone for one night without any interruptions?" exclaimed Greg.

"I'm about ready to be the rototiller bitch at the rate he keeps screaming," answered Charlotte as she started laughing.

Trunt was in bed laughing with his hand over his mouth and started screaming again. He was having fun waking up both parents in the middle of the night and making them come to his room. Suddenly, the door opened and once again it was his parents.

"Mommy, daddy, the rototiller bitch is here!"

Both parents looked at each other and looked irritated from the situation. They were beginning to think that something was going on.

"Listen to me," began Charlotte.

"This is not a game! Go to sleep or you'll be punished, do you understand?"

"I understand," answered Trunt. "I love you mommy."

"So no more screaming, waking up the dead," replied Greg.

Once again, both parents tucked their child into bed and walked back to their bedroom to get some sleep. Greg decided to turn in because of his day tomorrow and Charlotte was upset because she wanted to have sex.

Trunt sat in his bed and looked around at the walls. He suddenly felt scared and didn't want to be alone. He then heard a nightmarish sound in the closet that could only be interpreted as a motor. Trunt got out of bed and ran to the door to see what it was and opened it to see the nightmare creature herself.

"The rototiller bitch!" exclaimed Trunt as he screamed in terror.

"You called my name and here I am to take you away," she said.

The tall female creature had long black hair with blades of a rototiller on either side of her head. She also had blades mounted on her wrists.

"It's time for you to come with me," she growled as the blades began moving followed by the sound of a lawn mower.

Trunt let out a scream for help. Greg and Charlotte woke up, but this time they decided to stay in bed.

"No honey," began Greg, "He's got to learn that he can't play games."

Charlotte nodded and they went back to sleep. The rototiller bitch chased after Trunt and diced him into a million pieces with her rototiller blades before eating his heart. Blood was on the walls of the room before she left.

The next morning Charlotte knocked on Trunt's door with a tray of food. She knocked again and again. Then she turned the door knob to see blood all over the bed, walls and floor. Charlotte dropped the tray of food and let out a scream, which alerted Greg who was getting ready for work. He ran into the bedroom to see her crying, "the rototiller bitch ate our son!"

Fire Starter III: Bitter Sweet Revenge

It was mid-afternoon when Polly woke up. She found herself in a bath tub filled with gasoline. Thankfully she was still clothed, but her skin was burning like she was on fire and couldn't speak because her mouth was duct taped. Polly looked around to see she was in a bathroom and there was a young man staring out the window, but then turned to look at her.

The young man with sandy brown hair walked up to her and unpeeled the duct tape. He scooped some of the liquid out of the tub with a pale and put it in a small metal can before setting it on a tall stool.

"Now that you're awake I'll ask you some questions; do you know why you're here?"

Polly shook her head with fear as he lit a match and threw it in the can. He turned his head to look at her scared blue eyes.

Then fire bursted out of the can and she screamed, "please don't kill me."

"My name is Gary August and you're the social worker that was working on my child abuse case, do you remember?"

The lady began shaking her head and sobbed, "I handle thousands of cases every year how am I supposed to remember you!"

"Think Polly, twenty years ago when I was in fourth grade I was taken out of class. You were the social worker at the time and asked me if my parents spanked me. There were ten teachers involved in this case and it caused my parents to get a divorce. I was put into foster care because it was your recommendation to the judge. You ruined my life!" exclaimed Gary.

Polly's eyes widen as she remembered him, "oh my God! That was years ago, killing me won't justify the pain."

Gary looked at her angrily and began flicking his lighter on and off. He got up from the bath tub and walked out. She was scared and wondered what he was going to do to her.

Minutes went by and Polly began freaking out. Suddenly, a strange device was wheeled in by Gary. It was metal with hooks and it looked like something you would use to hold up meat from a butchered cow.

Polly began to freak out even more and screamed, but Gary laughed at her. He pulled the social worker out of the bath tub and lifted her up to a small seat.

"What are you going to do with me?" she cried.

Gary looked at her as he tied her legs down and her arms up. She could sense coldness from his face and knew it was too late to apologize. She knew he was going to kill her.

"You're going to give me the names of the prosecutor, judge and jury who were responsible for the destruction of my family those years ago."

"Oh God! I already told you I don't know," cried Polly. "Go ahead and kill me, you're just a killer!"

The twisted Fire Starter looked at her and turned to go to the medicine cabinet after she was restrained. Polly felt the circulation cut off from her arms and legs. Suddenly, Gary turned around with a couple of big needles.

"Not to worry, this won't kill you, but it will paralyze your limbs for about six hours."

"Are you sure you know what you're doing? What if it kills me?" she asked.

Gary walked over to her and injected the syringes into each of her limbs. He carefully pushed the needle into each nerve carefully so she would be numb. Polly began to feel dizzy and disembodied.

"Relax, this is just the beginning of the end," said Gary as he did one more injection before she fell unconscious.

Polly opened her eyes and still couldn't feel her limbs. She was naked, the feeling of discomfort in her armpits and crotch was driving her nuts. Polly turned her head to look around and started screaming in terror to her missing limbs and saw that she was hand stitched in the areas of where her body parts would have been.

Big metal hooks were stuck in her armpits and crotch. Gary was busy soaking something in the tub filled with gasoline. He turned around and smiled at the social worker.

"Well hello there, this is a surprise. Would you believe that you woke up two hours before your suppose to?"

"What the hell is this? What have you done to me?" she screamed.

"I disassembled your body and I'm soaking them in gasoline."

"Why don't you just kill me instead of torturing me?"

"Because I'm not finished with you," answered Gary.

"You're going to be a symbol of how you destroyed my family. I hate social workers, they always think they know everything," said Gary as he raised her leg from the tub.

"Gary listen to me carefully, the authorities will arrest you for murder and lock you up for life," said Polly.

Gary pulled out a flame thrower and a stream of fire shot out and hit the social worker. He watched the fire hit her face and chest as she screamed in pain. She moved her head back and forth quickly while feeling the burning sensation throughout her body.

"Go fuck yourself," replied Gary.

The Fire Starter walked up to her with a fire extinguisher and put the flames out. The social worker moaned in pain and started crying. Gary left the bathroom and came back with a pale of salt. He climbed up the stool and poured it over her wounds and then heard her scream. Then he left again and came back with a pale full of sand with fire ants and poured that on her as well. Gary took a step back and watched Polly jerk around frantically.

"Now you know what I had to go through while being cut off from my parents," yelled Gary as he flicked his lighter and threw it in the bathtub to burn her body parts and left.

"You're a bastard! Get back in here and finish me off I don't want to die by being eaten alive by fire ants!" screamed the social worker. Suddenly, the lights turned off; the door slammed shut with Polly screaming in agony while fire ants started eating her alive.

The Peddler's Dream

Vazeer woke up from his bed and turned around to see his six wives lying next to him, sleeping. Vazeer was a short little man that was sometimes mistaken as an elf or midget, but he was a peddler that traded goods for supplies and money. Vazeer tapped Krysta's shoulder and she woke up.

"Oh hi honey, last night was wonderful," she whispered.

"Can you cook me something to eat?" asked Vazeer in a whisper.

"Oh yes honey, anything for you," laughed Krysta. "What would you like?"

"Pancakes, eggs, sausage and cake, but make sure you have the other girls cook with you," said Vazeer.

"Hey after we clean and cook can we get a ten minute quickie?" asked Krysta.

"Yeah if you would shut up, you're always talking while we're making love and I lose my concentration," replied Vazeer.

"Oh please, oh please, I promise I'll be quiet. Can I be first before the other wives?"

Vazeer ignored her while walking out and got dressed to talk to Cougar, the talking cat that was sleeping outside in the porch on the swing. Vazeer woke him up and he rubbed his green eyes and fuzzy head. His ears perked up as he looked at his buddy Vazeer. Cougar was a big, fat, cat that was the size of a leopard.

"I had a dream I got molested," said Cougar.

"I've got a problem, my six wives are driving me crazy!"

"Well it's pretty obvious they don't want to have sex with me because I keep getting molested in my dreams."

Vazeer laughed and shook his head, "I really need some advice?"

"Be a pimp and make some money off of them," suggested Cougar.

"That's a good idea," replied Vazeer. "I'll continue to work as a peddler, sell my wood carvings, knick knacks and rent my wives out for pleasure!" laughed Vazeer as he rubbed his hands together.

"You want to rent me out ?" asked Cougar.

"Well, you never know. There might be somebody who maybe interested in beastly activities," smiled Vazeer.

"You should do something with Tree Frog," said Cougar.

Vazeer turned around to look at the man-dog sleeping in the cage on the porch. A man-dog was a crossbreed of a human and a dog. Unfortunately Tree Frog was the last of his kind and Vazeer saved him from being destroyed in an animal shelter.

Vazeer had a magical gift to talk to Tree Frog and nobody else could hear the man-dog. Tree Frog was becoming an annoyance and would constantly keep talking to him and wouldn't shut up. He would run around urinating everywhere, humping Big Ogla's leg, jumping on tables and becoming really obnoxious. Vazeer had to kick him outside, but then he would chase after Cougar and there were huge fights. Vazeer had no choice, but to stick him in the cage.

Vazeer awoke from his deep thought about Tree Frog and looked at Cougar. He was serious about how he was going to make money off of his wives and cover the taxes for the land. It was possible that he could teach Tree Frog some dog tricks like roll over, fetch, play dead and maybe even bark on command.

Then the door swung open and it was Big Olga. She was a young blonde girl that expected a lot out of Vazeer.

"Hey Vazeer your breakfast is done. Get in here and eat it, I can't be satisfied if you don't have any energy!" Big Olga ordered.

"Hey thanks!" yelled the peddler. "Get all the other wives together I've got an idea that will help us make more money."

"It better not involve Tree Frog and me because that creature should be killed," ordered Big Olga.

"No," said Vazeer.

"Will you rape me?" asked Cougar to the girl.

Vazeer started laughing as Big Olga took a deep breath and walked back inside. Vazeer was laughing so hard that his head was between his legs and Cougar could see his back pulsing with laughter.

"What's so funny? I guess that means no, right? Vazeer you got to help me, since you brought home Tree Frog I forgot the last time I got laid. I'm so horny I don't know what else to do. Can you help me get laid?" begged Cougar.

Vazeer scratched his head, "I don't know I could try. Who do you want me to send out to you?"

"Send me Big Olga or Kitten, I have a lot of fantasies about them. They make me so excited that I can't help myself?"

"Ewe, those are my wives you're talking about," answered Vazeer.

"I don't care! I would rather molest myself than to have sex with Tree Frog. "I'll talk to all six of my wives and explain to them what I would like them to do for me," replied Vazeer.

"Be careful, they might beat the crap out of you," warned Cougar.

Vazeer sat down at the big table with his six wives and looked at all of them. They seemed eager to hear what he had to say. Krysta was the talker, Big Olga was the dominant one, Nee Nah was the sweet one, Diana was the cleaner, Haley was the feisty one and then there was Kitten who was petite and loving.

"I asked you all to be assembled because I want you to work as my employees to get money for potential customers."

"What do you mean?" asked Diana.

"You want us to do what?" asked Nee Nah.

Vazeer was a little bit quiet as he looked at Big Olga. He could see she was getting angry and could already feel her kicking him between the legs.

"I was just thinking maybe you could show a wonderful night with another guy and get all the love you want so that you won't have to depend on me."

"We're not prostitutes, we're your wives," said Kitten.

"We've got to pay for the house, the land, our pet Cougar, Tree Frog the man-dog. I'm not making enough money selling my wooden sculptures."

"Cougar and Tree Frog are your problem, you shouldn't have fed them. They followed you home and now we can't get rid of them," replied Big Olga.

"You can practice on Cougar before I send you on your way," said Vazeer.

"Are you calling me a whore?" asked Big Olga as she stood up with her hands in a fist.

"Well if you practice now you can please a future customer," began Vazeer.

"Then we can get a repeat customer."

Big Olga turned red, rose up and started punching and kicking the midget. The other wives stayed out of it and watched. Then there was a knock at the door and Big Olga stopped kicking Vazeer in the face. Nee Nah answered the door and returned in a few seconds.

"It's Jem the warlock, he wants to talk to Vazeer."

Vazeer got up with a bloody nose and a black eye. He was in pain and wanted to escape from the house so he could re-think his strategy.

Vazeer approached the door and saw the hooded man with a dark robe. The robe was well designed in gold thread with the sun and moon. Jem took off the hood to reveal his long blonde hair and brown eyes. He raised the wooden charms and smiled at Vazeer.

"I would like you to make me a thousand of these and I'll pay you handsomely."

"Ok, but first I need your help to discipline my wives," begged Vazeer.

"Ok, what would you like done?"

"I don't know, I need some leverage so they won't beat the crap out of me or drain me in bed," replied Vazeer.

All of a sudden Tree Frog, the man-dog, broke out of his cage and began humping the warlock's leg. The warlock tried to shake him off, but the man-dog was gripped on tight. Vazeer turned his head to Cougar who was trying not to break out in laughter.

"What the hell is this creature?" asked Jem as he punched Tree Frog in the head. With the swing of his leg Tree Frog flung through the air and inside the kennel. Vazeer heard the man-dog crying and felt sorry for him, but then realized the warlock was here to help him.

"Please help me I want to be human," cried Tree Frog.

"You can threaten to call the rototiller bitch and she will kill your wives. Or I can put them under a spell and they will never harm you again. They will become the most beautiful creatures you have ever seen."

"How do I call the rototiller bitch?" asked the peddler.

"You just did, some have to call her three times, but I sense she will be at your house to kill your wives and give you free time to work for me."

"But what if I need to get laid?" cried Vazeer.

"Wives are easy to replace as a donkey," laughed the warlock as he left to go to his carriage.

The Peddler walked with Jem to his black carriage with twelve donkeys in front. Vazeer scratched his head as he thought; *what did I get myself into now?*

"Now begin my project," ordered the warlock. "And your wives shall never bother you again."

The peddler took a deep breath but before he got in his courage, Cougar walked up to the warlock and stared at him, "can you molest me?"

Jem's eyes turned red and Cougar backed away. The warlock climbed up to his carriage and left. Vazeer covered his mouth to keep from laughing.

"Did you talk to Big Olga or Kitty about me getting laid?" asked Cougar.

"Yeah and I got beat up," replied Vazeer.

"Then I guess the answer is no."

Vazeer didn't say anything because his mind was already preoccupied as to how he was going to make a thousand little wood sculptures without having to satisfy his wives for a night. Then when he walked back inside he saw a parrot cage and six fairies resembling his wives inside. He didn't have to worry about being harassed, hearing drama or getting beat up.

Vazeer sat down and decided to take a nap. So off to bed he went, but unfortunately he had nightmares, rolled off the bed and out of sight. Cougar and Tree Frog snuck in the house because a thunderstorm was coming and wanted to get away from the rain. They jumped on the bed and fell asleep.

That night a great evil crept inside the house. It was the rototiller bitch and she grabbed each screaming fairy and ate them. She walked into the bedroom hoping to find the one who called her name and thought it was the two strange creatures on the bed. Right away they woke up after hearing a loud noise that sounded like motor and she slit their necks with her spinning blades that were on her wrists. Blood sprayed on the bed, the walls and expensive clothing, but after searching the house for more occupants she ate Cougar and Tree Frog, then she left inside the closet that she had entered from.

The next morning Vazeer woke up on the floor from the other side of the bed to find blood on his face and all over the room. He stepped through the house to find his wives were gone. Then he heard a knock at the door and when he answered, it was Jem.

"Have you finished creating my pieces?" asked the warlock.

"I didn't have time, something destroyed my home and murdered my family. There's blood all over the place!" exclaimed Vazeer.

"You are going to be changed into something for not doing my work!" yelled the warlock.

"Please don't turn me into a man-dog!" cried Vazeer.

"Oh no, I'm going to change you into something far worse," he laughed as he raised his hands.

Vazeer woke up to find himself in an aquarium. It was all a bad dream and now his master Tree Frog was petting him. Tree Frog was talking to six girls in his room and a strange man who looked identical to the man in his dream. There was a house cat sitting on the boy's bed that resembled Cougar and the small rodent took a deep breath of relief and was grateful that it was only a dream.

Anna Cabeca

"You whore!" yelled Narkeeta "Get out here and clean the living room!"

The girl he was yelling at was his wife, Ceara. She had blue eyes, dark blonde hair and wore a common brown dress. Ceara was upset that their marriage was not what she thought it was going to be. Narkeeta was an average man; handsome and in the beginning was very kind, but then he became a slave master.

It wasn't fair to be abused, but it seemed that was her purpose in life, which was to bare his cruelty and give birth to his children. She felt like an ass, but it was only because he made her feel like it. Ceara was keeping something from Narkeeta, she had a dark secret that made her different than other women.

It was written in the land of Zha that for two people to be together, secrets were forbidden. Ceara was scared to tell him her secret because she couldn't control it.

Ceara picked up the living room and was busy washing dishes. She felt broken in spirit because her life was in stagnation. He smiled whenever she would bend over to pick up his socks and when he was finished drinking his goblet of beer. He would purposely drop it on the floor. It fell on the rug and Ceara looked at it and then at him. Narkeeta raised his eyebrow and gestured her to pick it up. Ceara bent over to pick it up and he slapped her ass. Ceara rose up quickly and watched him laugh at her.

"That's very ill mannered!" she exclaimed, but all he did was laugh at her.

"Tonight you will fulfill your purpose to me. I'm going to pop you and you shall have my child."

Ceara's heart began to beat faster and she could hear it thump louder in her chest. She was getting upset and could feel her blood boil, but she calmed down and hoped that it would subside.

"You will not pop me because if you do I will turn into Anna Cabeca!"

"Yeah right," he replied and he slapped her in the face.

He got up from his chair; quickly grabbed her long brown hair and dragged her into the bedroom. There were lots of noises all night and then they ceased.

The next morning Narkeeta opened the bedroom door and walked out. Ceara slowly walked out bruised and touched her herself between the legs. She touched herself because she was in a lot of pain and began crying. It was a rough night, much rougher than previous nights.

Narkeeta walked out of the bedroom and sat at the table, "cook me breakfast, now! Woman!"

Quickly Ceara began getting the ingredients together. Then she realized that she didn't know what he wanted to eat.

"What do you want to eat?"
"Eggs of course, foolish woman"

She lit a match to start a fire on the stove and pulled out a cast iron frying pan and placed it over the fire. After putting some butter in the pan she heard her husband laughing at her, but ignored him and cracked an egg in the pan. He continued to laugh at her and Ceara turned her head to him and wondered what was so funny.

"You thought you could deny me by threatening me with Anna Cabeca!"

Ceara ignored him, but felt her body begin to boil as she wanted to kill him. She continued to break the eggs and after they cooked Ceara served him. Ceara hoped that if she treated him well that he would be nice.

That evening he did the same thing as before and dropped his goblet of beer on the rug in the living room. Ceara walked over to pick it up and he slapped her on the ass.

"That's very ill mannered," she said.

"Tonight you will fulfill your purpose to me. I'm going to pop you and you shall have my child."

Ceara's heart began to pump faster and she could hear it pump louder in her chest. She wanted to turn into Anna Cabeca right there, but she thought about the first moment he kissed her and the life they built together.

"You will not pop me because if you do I will turn into Anna Cabeca!"

"Yeah right," he replied and he slapped her face.

He got up from his fat chair; quickly grabbed her long hair and dragged the girl into the bedroom. There were lots of noises all night and then they ceased.

The third day of their marriage Ceara was getting tired of it and that evening when Narkeeta got drunk and dropped his goblet of beer on the floor. She didn't pick it up and stood there looking at him. His wife wanted to hear what he was going to say. Narkeeta looked at her and gestured her to pick it up, but she shook her head slowly.

"Pick it up, that's your purpose," he demanded.

Ceara grabbed her coat and was putting it on just as she reached for the door. Narkeeta got up and stopped her, by standing in the way. Ceara was trapped and she was getting upset with him. Her eyes suddenly turned yellow and hair grew on her arms and hands.

"Tonight you will fulfill your purpose to me. I'm going to pop you and you shall have my child!"

"You will not pop me because if you try I will turn into Anna Cabeca!" she said with a growl.

She could hear her heart pump and felt an adrenaline rush. Then she noticed her teeth began to grow longer as well as her fingernails.

Narkeeta looked at her strangely, "why do you look like a dog?"

Suddenly, Ceara lost her temper and growled at him like a wolf. He tried to grab her neck, but she quickly grabbed his hands and twisted them off. She smiled when he cried in pain. Then with four swipes of her claws he fell to the floor and blood was everywhere. She got on top of him; busted his jaw and ripped his ribcage apart.

The next morning Ceara opened up the oven to check on her meal. It was roast beef with potatoes, carrots and peas. With a sharp knife she cut into the meat to see it was still pink. It would still need a few minutes.

"Not quite the way I like it, but at least my husband will fulfill his purpose to me. I tried to warn him about Anna Cabeca, but he wouldn't listen," she chuckled to herself and closed the oven.

Healing Heart II: A Healed Broken Heart

Wes sat in his car seat as the Kia drove really fast down the street. They were almost to the exit that led to the freeway. Annie reached her hand to the radio to change the station and then smiled at Wes.

Wes smiled back and looked at her tattoos on her arms. There was so much of her that he remembered from the barn dance and how much they talked on the telephone and the memories bombarded him.

Suddenly, they passed the mountains that were miles away from the freeway and Wes' mouth dropped. He couldn't believe how beautiful she looked. Wes turned his head to look at Seilah and Haden who were quiet in their seats. He smiled at them and they smiled back.

They made it back to Annie's apartment and Wes looked around to see it was a nice day. The apartment was dark inside because the drapes covered the windows, but it was nice and cozy. Wes turned on the light and looked around at the lived in apartment. Annie checked her messages and got on the phone.

Seilah was eating some chips, "I can open up my

mouth really wide want to see?"

Wes watched Seilah opened her mouth and smiled. She was cute and full of life.

"Seilah close your mouth, that's gross," said Annie while she continued to talk on the phone.

"Do you want to play Connect Four or Candy Land?" asked Seilah.

"Sure let's play Candy Land," he answered with a laugh.

Wes remembered the game when he was a kid, but when Seilah pulled out the board game he saw that it was different and was a little disappointed. He didn't like changes, but realized changes were necessary to grow and move on.

Annie got off the phone and saw that Wes was playing a board game with her kids. She walked over and sat down to observe. Everyone was laughing and having fun together playing the board game. Wes looked at Annie while smiling and saw that she was looking a little dim, but a smile emerged when she saw Wes looking at her.

"Is everything ok?" he asked.

"Everything is fine," she answered. "I was thinking that tomorrow we could go to the Garden of the Gods."

"Ok," replied Wes.

The afternoon went into the evening of playing board games and Annie put the kids to bed. They were alone and eating her barbeque ribs that she prepared when they got home. It was so good Wes's mouth began to water as soon as he saw the plate in front of him.

"This looks really good," he complemented.

"Thanks," she smiled as she continued eating

her food. "I'm exhausted and going to bed. You should probably get some sleep as well. Hiking on the trails can get exhausting and you'll need all the sleep you can get."

Wes nodded his head understanding, "is it all right if I stay up to watch a little television?"

"Sure, just keep the volume down," Annie answered as she left to go to her room.

Wes stayed up as he flipped through channels all night and couldn't find anything interesting to watch. He was thinking of a prior relationship with another girl named Arrisa. Arrisa was a girl he met on the internet and the relationship ended badly under a misunderstanding.

He turned off the television and turned to see the books on the shelf. He rummaged through one particular book of unexplained mysterious. One mystery he read was about cats born with wings. As he read on, he found himself drifting asleep and slowly closed his eyes.

Wes walked around a desolate land filled with mountains. He looked up to see a large dark red sun and a red sky with no clouds. He could see he was in a town where nobody was around. Red fire was on the buildings, but they weren't burning. Wes became scared when he realized he was in Hell and looked around in the distance to see demons on the buildings.

After looking around, he saw a black cat, with wings of a raven, and it hiss at him and then it ran into the gas station. Wes couldn't believe what he was seeing and decided to walk into the gas station to get a better look at the animal. Then before he got in the door Arrisa walked outside to meet him. She looked weathered; her appearance was a mess from the pretty face she once had. When Wes knew her she was a beautiful blonde with brown eyes and a gorgeous smile. As strange as it was to see her Wes saw beautiful white wings on her back.

"Wes I'm so glad you're here!" she gasped with delight and hugged him followed with a kiss.

"Arrisa, what are you doing here?" he asked.

"The devil took me away from my room. He locked me away in this place until I serve him, please save me and take me with you!"

Wes stopped hugging her and backed away while hearing strange screechy noises that sounded like birds.

"Don't you love me?" she asked.

"I did."

"Will you save me," she began crying.

"Um, no."

"Why?" she cried.

"Because you fucked me over."

"But I didn't mean it," she cried and reached for him.

Wess looked at her like she was on crack and backed away, "Get away from me."

Suddenly, there was a huge shake in the land. Wes looked around and saw lots of demons creeping on the roof of the gas station. They looked like lizard humanoid bat people . They had horns on their heads, red skin and leather wings.

Wes backed away even more and saw them walking out from behind the lifeless cars and debris that was lying all over the ground. Arrisa began screaming out his name while running out to him. Wes watched helplessly as five demons jumped on her and raped her before ripping her body apart.

*"Wes save me! I love you!" she
screamed her last breath and lied motionless as
the demons feasted on her corpse.*

*Wes saw the creatures take notice of
him and walked towards him. He turned around
to see he was surrounded by them and saw a
large demon emerge from the crowd of
thousands. The demon grabbed Wes, while
opening its mouth to take a bite out of his face.
Wes watched in fright and let out a scream.*

Wes woke up in a cold sweat and realized it was just a dream. He took a deep breath as he saw the light was on and looked at the floor to see the book on the floor. The book he was reading showed a picture of a black cat with wings. He couldn't understand why Arrisa was in his dream asking to be saved? Wes closed the book and shut the light off to lie on the couch. He stared at the ceiling and waited for Annie to wake up.

The next morning Wes and Annie left for the Garden of the Gods. It was a beautiful park with mountains and bike trails, walking trails and beautiful flowers. Seilah and Hayden were being baby sat by her mom and they were alone on a mountain having a picnic.

"You're awfully quiet," said Annie.

Wes turned his head from looking at the mountains ahead and smiled at her. He didn't want to ruin the moment by talking about Arrisa or the nightmare. He wanted to make things work between them.

"I'm just enjoying the view. There's a lot of beauty in Colorado," he replied.

"Are you thinking about moving here?" she asked.

Wes looked around the landscape and realized he had a huge decision to make. He could have a life living in Colorado and potentially have a love affair with Annie or to remain in Wisconsin with the support of friends and family. It was true that they talked on the phone everyday about getting together. It seemed imaginable to attain and wondered what it would be like?

He was a designer and working a dead end job at the newspaper press in a weak economy. Wes continued to try and would keep trying until he would hit the success desired. He was motivated with nothing holding him back from accomplishing his dreams.

Annie was divorced with two children and was going to college. On the phone it was clear she was tied down with the responsibilities for her children and couldn't leave Colorado even if she wanted to. They lived different lifestyles and had opposite responsibilities to perform. Annie wanted a man, she wanted to fall in love and have a family. She loved Wes and wanted to be with him. Wes kept finding women that wanted to go out drinking, get laid and move on. This was a sure thing that they both had for each other and it would work.

Wes turned his head and looked at her with a smile. "I was just thinking what else is out here?"

Annie got up from sitting on the rock and sat next to him, "more trails, more adventure."

"I want to see more of this ," Wes replied and watched a smile emerge on her face.

"Then let's go before the sun sets," she laughed.

After four days of fun, Wes could see a change

come over him as he realized he was beginning to fall for her. They went on many hikes and picnics together until they explored every passage. Wes was sitting in his chair while they drove, thinking about what to do next. He was listening to a good song on the radio when suddenly Annie changed the radio station.

"I liked that song," he said.

Annie turned it back to the song on the radio station. Wes continued his train of thought as the music relaxed him. Then as soon as the song was over she began channel surfing again and Wes looked at her puzzled.

"What?" she asked.

"Why do you do that?"

"So I don't miss a good song."

"Yeah, but you're missing all the good songs that will come on next."

They drove through town and went inside a little gift shop that had dragons, angels, fairies and crystals. It was a magical place and Wes could hear the soft angelic voice of Celtic music playing from the speakers.

After walking around and making purchases, they left to go to the park. Seilah and Haden played on the swings with Annie while Wes sat at the picnic table with a notebook. Ann turned around to see that he was writing something.

"What are you writing?" she asked with a smile. Wes looked at her and smiled, "it's a short story I started."

"A short story, what is it about?"

"It's about vampires and angels," he answered while looking at her and could see something was bothering her. "What's the matter?"

"A lot of things are on my mind," she replied.

"Like what?"

"When you live a stressful life of worry you let me know how you feel," said Ann

Wes was quiet and felt her pain, suddenly before anything could be said Seilah interrupted, "can we go home now, I want to play Connect Four with Wes."

"Yes, baby we're leaving right now, but we have to stop off at the library."

"That's great I have to check my email," replied Wes.

"Yes, but we can't be in there long," said Ann.

"Ok, how long were you thinking?" he asked.

"A few minutes maybe ten minutes at the most," she replied while getting up.   "Hayden, come on, it's time to go," said Annie as they walked back to the car.

Wes began thinking about Annie and then Arrisa as they drove away in the Kia. A girl like Annie was someone with a heart of gold and a beautiful soul that could be loved well, but with a past of sadness. Could this work? Then of course there was Arrisa, the girl from the internet who was beautiful in every way with a life built around being devoted to her man. She had a lot of problems of being needy to him.

Arrisa was gone with only the memories, dreams and the sound of her voice. If Arrisa truly wanted him in her life she would have kept in contact. Annie was right in front of him, waiting, and all he had to do was take their relationship further. Wes closed his eyes and drifted asleep.

Wes walked around the desolate land filled with mountains. He looked up to see a large dark red sun and a red sky with no clouds. He could see he was in the same place where

nobody was around. Red fire was on the buildings, but they weren't burning. Wes took a deep breath as a flutter of emotions took hold of him. He knew he was dreaming and began thinking of Arrisa.

After looking around and feeling lonely he saw a black cat with the wings of a raven hiss at him and then it ran into the gas station. Wes recognized it from before and followed it into the gas station to get a better look at it. Then before he got in the door Arrisa walked outside to meet him. She looked the same as before; her appearance was a mess from when he first met her.

When Wes knew her she was a beautiful blonde with brown eyes and a gorgeous smile. As strange as it was to see her, Wes saw beautiful white wings on her back.

"Wes I'm so glad you're here!" she gasped with delight and hugged him followed with a kiss.

"Arrisa, what are you doing here?" he demanded.

"The devil brought me here. He locked me up in this place until I agree to serve him, please save me and take me with you!" Wes stopped hugging Arrisa and backed away, while looking at her then she stared at his chest.

Wes suddenly felt a huge pain in his chest and looked down to see blood spill out of his heart. Wes looked at Arrisa as she looked at him innocently then smiled at him. For some reason he could sense that she was a part of this pain he was feeling.

"What's going on with my heart?" he asked while gasping for air.

Then Arrisa move closer to him as she licked her lips, "you are a good man and I want your heart."

Without warning an arrow shot into Arrisa. The person was dressed in tight leather with long black hair and black wings like a raven. The heroin was Ann and she looked at Wes. She fired her crossbow at Arrisa again, shot her in the chest and died then she looked at the emerging demons from behind the cars.

Wes felt weak and collapsed to the ground. He tried to get up, but got a quick gesture from Ann with her hand to be still. She looked at him with kindness and ripped the front part of his shirt where blood was coming out of his chest. He felt her tongue lick the wound and then her entire mouth suck the blood. It was a strange sensation and he kind of liked it because it didn't hurt. He felt like he was healing and opened his eyes while looking into hers and heard her say, "everything is going to be ok."

Wes opened his eyes and realized that they had just pulled in the parking lot at the library. It seemed quick and easy to get from the mountains to town. They walked inside and right away Wes got on a computer that would allow him to be on there for fifteen minutes. As soon as he was finished, he looked around for Ann and saw she got on a computer that lasted an hour. After waiting for what seemed to be twenty minutes he walked up to her station.

"Are we ready to go?" he asked.

"Yeah just a minute, I've got to check my other messages."

Wes politely left and kept an eye on her kids until she was finished. They waited outside in the shade under a tree from the sun. He thought about the last four days of their conversation and then the dreams. He thought he knew what he wanted, but was uneasy because he was partly scared about moving in with her. He could feel a strange repelling feeling from her whenever he got close and it was opposite than what he expected. He couldn't help, but feel he was being taken advantage somehow, but Annie was his friend.

The channel surfing and tricking him out of spending more time on the internet was impolite. He wanted to be in love with her, but it seemed like it was an uphill journey.

After an hour, Annie walked out of the library and everyone joined together at the car to go home. They went cruising down the street and across the intersection while Annie channel surfed the radio from one song to the next. Wes could recognize the pattern of turning the dial on the stereo, which was like moving from one relationship to the next without thinking about the consequences.

They arrived at her apartment and once again had to deal with the complete darkness. Right away Wes turned on the lights and Annie checked her messages. After watching TV and playing Connect Four with Seilah the day drew to a close. Annie tucked the kids into bed.

It was her birthday and they celebrated by having a few drinks and watched a vampire movie. After a few hours they played music by George Michael and talked about how much fun they had together.

"Let's dance," smiled Wes.

"I don't know, dancing for me is a sacred thing, it's like having sex," she replied.   As reluctant as she was he was able to move with her to the sound of

George Michael and he looked into her eyes.

"I don't think you're serious about moving out here," she said.

"Why?" he asked.

"My kids drive me crazy. I promise you that once you get back on that bus you'll feel relieved."

"Your kids can't be that bad," he answered.

"I think you would be happier with someone else. If I was a guy I wouldn't go out with me."

Wes held her close and felt her pain, it was an emotional pain deep down. He turned his head and kissed her. She looked at him surprised as though trying to figure out why he did that.

"Why did you do that?" she asked.

Wes looked at her and then stopped dancing, realizing that she was living the same torment that he was. Broken hearts from relationships of the past that was making things difficult to move on. They looked into each other's eyes and it seemed that they were reading each other's mind and knew what they wanted to do.

Annie turned off the lights in the living room and they both walked into her room. He held her close and kissed the back of her neck and felt her trembling. In his dream she rescued him from his pain and suffering by sucking the blood from the wound in his heart. He closed his eyes and felt her lips touch his neck. Her fingernails scratched his back and he ran his fingers through her soft black hair.

"You're an amazing woman," he whispered, but all he got was a coy look in her eyes. He picked her up while walking to the bed to lie down together and they made out all night.

The next morning Wes woke up on her bed and the blinds were up to reveal the sun. It was an amazing change to take place and Wes looked around to see he was alone. He saw her Twilight books on the shelf and remembered how interested she was in being a vampire.

He walked outside her room to the living room and saw the kids watching television. The blinds on the windows were open and he saw, through the window, Annie outside. Her back was turned and it looked like she was in deep thought.

Wes began to walk across the living room to talk to her when he was stopped by Seilah, "want to play Connect Four?"

"Maybe later," he smiled as he walked outside to see her.

"Hi," he said.

Right away Annie turned her head and smiled at him, "hi."

"I would like to thank you for having me visit."

"Life is full of lessons," said Ann.

Right away Wes had an idea for a saying that emerged in his mind. *Love is more than a feeling, it's a lesson to help you on your way.* Ann had helped free him from thinking about Arrisa and now he was ready to move on with his life.

It was time for Wes to leave and Ann pulled up to the bus in the Kia and walked with him to assist him by getting his stuff together. It seemed nostalgic because the vacation went so fast and they met each other for the first time in fifteen years. Wes hugged his soulmate and watched her get back into the car. The Kia took off and Wes walked into the bus station by himself. He turned around realizing that she didn't stick around, she wasn't interested in him as a boyfriend or a husband. She wasn't really in love with him and serious to have him move in with her to begin with.

The bus pulled up and he got on, took a seat, pulled out a pencil and paper. He continued writing his short story, "The Vampire and the Angel".

He had the inspiration from Ann to finish it. Then he heard a familiar song from Amy Grant and began to laugh. He realized that fate was teaching him a lesson about his life, and his pen pal, Ann.

The Vampire and the Angel

Dedicated to Kisus.

For five thousand years, dark evil creatures rose from the underworld and slaughtered all that was good that lived in harmony on the land. It became known as the dark ages and no human could be found.

On the coast of the continent known as Copper Toe lived a vampire named Kissa who was collecting sea shells. She looked like a human girl of about seventeen years of age, she was five foot ten and one-hundred and thirty pounds with white skin, black hair and blue eyes. She lived alone in her cottage; inside the dingy brown village called Eneema with other vampires.

The sun was in a constant eclipse for the last five thousand years and food was scarce. Humans were becoming rare to find and vampires were at war with wear-wolves, eyeresettes, gargoyles, zombies, gothicas, fallens and sometimes other vampire clans.

After spending most of the day collecting sea shells and filling up her wooden pail with them, Kissa ran from the beach onto the grass. She carefully walked through the woods, carrying her bucket of sea shells when suddenly she heard something.

Kissa heard the sound of a baby crying nearby and wondered if it was a human. The vampire set the bucket down and followed the sound until she came across the creature making the sound in the tall grass.

Her eyes feasted upon the naked flesh of a baby, about a year old, in a white silk blanket. Immediately her mouth watered and when she opened it to smile, her fangs emerged. Then something peculiar could be seen on the baby's back and they were wings similar to a bird.

Kissa realized while she touched its wings that the baby was an angel. Her hands felt a break in the right wing and it needed mending.

The vampire's fangs retracted and she smiled at the baby so that it wouldn't scream and cry. She heard about angels through stories and knew that they were extremely rare to see, let alone catch.

The baby angel stopped crying and looked at her with his amazing aqua blue eyes. He began to laugh and reached for her long black hair to touch it as it fell on his body. Kissa looked at the baby and decided to nurture it back to health.

The other vampires would immediately kill the angel and drink its blood if she reported it. If there was one thing vampires loved more was the blood of an angel. It was sweet and full of energy, which was a hundred times stronger than the vitality of a human. She covered the baby in the white blanket and held it against her chest with her left arm. She could hear the baby purring and smiled as she picked up the pale of shells with her right hand to make the journey home.

The village of Eneema was a dingy brown colored town that was tasteless and old. Kissa could feel the baby's weight increase and used her vampire senses to avoid other vampires that would be a threat. She didn't want the angel to get eaten by her kin.

Once she got in the house; Kissa set the baby on the table, lit some candles to see her plants were dying. She ignored them and took off the white blanket to see the baby had grown into a child of about five years old.

Kissa gasped with a surprise as she saw the angel's hair was sterling silver in color with white skin and looked like a beautiful little girl. The angel child let out a strange bird sound that sounded beautiful. She smelled a sweet odor and it was almost hard to keep away. The smell was lilacs, apples, honey and sugar combined.

"What is your name?" she asked aloud while touching the child's face, which was a straight face.

The child looked away and then back at her with a smile. Then almost immediately, Kissa had a picture in her head of when she was human falling from the sky and being caught by a handsome muscular man.

"Is your name Catch?"

The little angel smiled as a light purr grew louder from him. This purr was similar to a sea gull or a cat and Catch nodded his head to her. She smiled at how cute he was and felt like a mentor to this little person.

Kissa took a step towards the angel; touched the broken wing and heard him cry in pain. She immediately let go as her eyes well up with tears, the vampire's hands began trembling when she felt the pain. The angel touched his right wing with his hands and looked at the vampire sadly.

"I'm sorry," she cried.

She knew that when humans broke a bone they needed to be bandaged in order for the healing to begin. It became apparent that the angel's wing needed to be bandaged in order for it to heal effectively. Angels were magical, so why wasn't it healing on its own? She asked herself.

Kissa began digging around her home, looking for something to tie to the broken wing. She found a stick, a towel and began mixing some paper mesh with water.

"Bare with me child and let me help you," she said tenderly while taking the mud and touched the angel's broken wing.

The angel cried in pain as she held the broken wing and tied it with the stick. She then held the plaster like substance until it was completely dry and hard. The angel was quiet and looked at her before it began making the purr sound again.

Kissa smiled and had a strange sensation in her chest. It couldn't have been a heart developing in her dead body, but none the less she was beginning to feel different. The vampire suddenly heard the sound of blow horn and knew that there was a meeting being called.

She turned to look at the angel, "stay here, I'll be right back."

Kissa walked to the middle of the village where their vampire leader Kaveezeer, was talking. He was the oldest, strongest and wisest of the vampires. He was the first vampire to set up the town, organize the first group of vampires and appointed who the warriors would be. There were only about five-hundred vampires in Eneema. Other clans were many miles away and cities of vampires were spread out.

"I'm happy to say that we've been able to protect our borders well from the wear-wolves. I'm still very concerned about the gothicas who eat vampires. Leaders from the cities have sent a message for us to disband and return to the cities. I've not answered the message because I believe that we should come first. We may be small, but I believe that we have the strength to defend our land!"

Kissa looked around at all the vampires who cheered and clapped their hands. Kaveezeer was unlike the typical leader who only cared about himself and socializing with other vampires in Eneema. In this dark time it was difficult to know which side to be on. Vampires would often turn on other vampires while wear-wolves would be allies with other vampire clans to over throw leaders and armies. Eyeresettes would take the sides of gargoyles and fallens would side with dark fairies. These groups would take sides to overthrow certain powers and take over territory. For five thousand years there was nothing, but violence and hatred in each of the different races of the dead and beasts.

Kissa wiped her eyes from the thought of constant war, but was also thinking about herself as well as the feelings she harbored. She continued to listen with the other vampires of what their leader proposed, which was to remain a rogue town. After a few hours of listening she decided to leave so that she could check on the angel.

When she got back home; she looked around for Catch and found the angel sitting in the living area with his back facing her. His hands were clasped together and the sound of singing emanated from him that sounded like fairies. Kissa walked around to see his face and realized the angel was older, about thirteen years old. He was still naked and his skin was white with sterling, silver hair stretching to the middle of his back.

Kissa's eyes began to turn from dark blue to light blue. She was hungry, but fought the temptation to attack the angel. Catch opened his now crystal blue eyes and smiled at her. He rose up from the floor and was a half a foot shorter than her.

"What were you doing?" she asked.

The angel didn't answer and only purred like a kitten. She received pictures in her head of an orb of light intensely bright that it blinded her. Kissa then felt a question enter such mind and it was a picture of her sleeping.

The vampire smiled and began to laugh to such a coy question, "vampires don't sleep."

Then without a warning she received a hug from him and a kiss upon such lips that overburdened her with emotion. It was moist as well as sweet just like his smell and she began to feel a weight in her knees. First her eyelids began to get heavy and her knees became weak.

"This is ridiculous, I'm not getting tired and I'm not falling in love with you, you're just a child!" she exclaimed. The angel only looked at her with his loving eyes and nodded his head with assurance that everything would be ok.

"What have you done to me? Vampires don't get tired!" she said with a yawn and began to sit up on the couch.

The angel fetched a blanket and pillows to make it more comfortable for her to sleep. Kissa tried to sit up on the couch and was feeling the effects of fatigue. For so many years she was in control and looked up at the angel who was looking down upon her like the child. Her eyes closed as she slipped into a deep sleep.

She *was falling through the sky and landed on the ground. She got up and looked around to see her clan fighting wear-wolves, eyeresettes, gargoyles, and fallens. It was a losing battle because these creatures were killing her kin, but she didn't care about that.*

She walked to her house and stepped inside to see it was lit by candles and Catch was in the living room. He was the same age as she remembered and he was looking at her sad.

221

Kissa smelled his scent and couldn't help herself. She charged and jumped on top of him as she bit his neck. He cried like a baby deer while she drank his blood and ripped large chunks of flesh with her teeth. She rose her head up and realized that the angel's odor was really strong. It was like eating an apple and running out of skin. The vampire could see the inside of his body was white, but there was no apple core. She couldn't resist her urge and ate every bodypart of the angel until he was completely gone. Kissa then heard a knock at the door and answered it to see wear-wolves, eyeresettes, gargoyles and fallens looking at her and saw bodies of decapitated vampires on the ground. Tears emerged from Kissa's eyes as she cried for the loss of her kin.

Kissa woke up from her nightmare and took deep breaths as she looked around to see her plants were looking a little better. Catch was kneeled down on a rug that was on the hardwood floor and was praying. He looked a little bit older and his body was becoming muscular. She also saw her shells in the bucket were removed and tied together on a string in the form of necklaces.

The bandage on the angel's wing was holding well and she watched the angel's eyes open to look at her. Catch smiled at her as she got up from the couch and suddenly heard a voice in her head. *Did you sleep well?*

"No I didn't sleep well, vampires don't sleep because we don't get vitality to rest our bodies.

What did you dream about?

Kissa looked at him and hesitated before speaking, "you really want to know?"

The angel smiled while nodding his head and Kissa told him her dream. Catch looked at Kissa and nodded his head with understanding.

After Kissa told Catch her dream there was a pause and a strange silence from both of them. Catch looked a little frustrated as though that wasn't his intention, but he was beginning to understand that vampires were different from humans.

"Look this is what I am and I've had to accept this for thousands of years. Being a dark person doesn't mean I'm evil. I still love nature, animals and plants but I can never be the way I was before, I've changed."

The angel looked sad and confused; he wasn't quite sure what to do next. Kissa began to sulk and let out a sigh, "Catch, why did you come here?" There was a silence for a minute and then she heard his voice in her head.

I crashed and reverted as a baby. Then you saved me and I matured. You saved me Kissa!

"That's not what I mean, why did I find you near the beach with a broken wing? Why didn't you crash somewhere else?"

There are no words to describe what my reasoning is and I can't tell you because I'm forbidden too.

"You're in love with me that much is clear," declared Kissa.

Love is more than a feeling, it's a lesson to help you on your way.

Kissa was getting hungry and walked out to her goat farm. Vampires were now domesticating animals so they wouldn't starve. Catch watched through the window as Kissa walked into the pin and attacked one of the goats. She bit its neck, drank its blood and the angel could hear the animal cry for help. After killing eight of the goats and leaving their bodies to lie in the pen, the angel walked into the living area and kneeled on the rug to meditate.

When Kissa came back into her house from feeding she looked at the angel who was sitting on the couch and wiped the blood from her mouth. She felt a little embarrassed because of the way he looked at her. It was the look of shame and it was very uncomfortable to accept from the angel.

"Why are you looking at me that way?"

Where I come from it's not normal for creatures to drink the blood of another.

"Well, this is the way I am and I enjoy drinking blood," she replied while walking to the sofa and sat down next to the angel.

"How's your broken wing?" she asked trying to change the subject, but only got a slow shake from his head that followed with the uncomfortable silence that went on for the next few minutes.

"Look, I'm sorry that you're offended by my behavior of sucking blood. Why don't you share with me a piece of what your life is like?"

Catch looked at her and was a little hesitant, but then after a few minutes he nodded his head. He gestured her to face him and he placed his hands on her face. Kissa closed her eyes and felt his fingers and thumb on the base of her skin.

Kissa suddenly was in his world and looked around to see how beautiful it was. She looked up at the clouds to see rings around the world she was in. There were multiple moons and a silver sun that remained constant in the sky. There was vibrant green grass loaded with flowers that were littered on the ground. Kissa looked at her hands to see her skin was peach in color. She walked around and came across a wide river. The river was light blue with white sand on the bottom and she looked into it to see herself that could be described as her soul. She couldn't believe how beautiful she was. It was so powerful that Kissa began to cry because she never knew how beautiful her soul was.

The vampire turned around after hearing the sound of music and followed it. It was beautiful and after walking through the forest she looked to the sight of strange creatures playing instruments. There were two angels; one was playing piano while the other was playing a harp. Two other angelic creature, were playing musical instruments. One was playing the flute while the other was playing a . Kissa looked around to see more creatures that looked like Catch. They were hard to distinguish, but they joined together in a choir and their voices mixed together like the sound of morning noise after the rain had fallen.

Kissa opened her eyes and felt relaxed and saw all the plants in the house were becoming healthy. She was happy to get a glimpse of the angel world, but then her heart began to flutter with fear when Catch was nowhere in sight. The vampire looked around and heard something in the pen where she kept her goats. Immediately, she thought it was another vampire trying to rob her and ran outside to see.

To surprise the angel was in the pen with the goats. Her mouth dropped to see that the angel brought the goats back to life. The angel was no longer naked and had what looked like a long night gown that covered his body.

He was kneeled down to the last goat and held his hand over the goat's neck. Within minutes the goat woke up and walk around. Catch smiled as all the goats swarmed around him like bees to honey. They were kissing and licking the angel's face with their tongues, giving him their gratitude. Catch cracked a grin as his wings spread apart. Then he let out a light cry for his right wing hadn't completely healed yet and both wings returned back to it's normal fold.

Kissa began to cry and wiped her cheeks from the tears that fell from such eyes. She killed the goats to satisfy her hunger and was stealing their lives right in front of them. It was now understood why the angel frowned upon what she wa
s doing, but how else was she to survive? She loved the angel and the angel loved her, but how were they to have a loving relationship? The answer was simple; they could never have a lasting relationship and he was right in what was said. Love is more than a feeling; it's a lesson to help you on your way.

Kissa walked over to the pin and the angel looked at her with a smile. She looked around outside and knew it was night because the eclipsed sun was nowhere in sight, leaving the stars to sparkle. She was scared that other vampires were outside and Catch was risking his life.

"You did what I couldn't do," she began. "You gave them life after I took it from them."

Kissa smiled and looked into his eyes as she realized there was something admirable about Catch that it made her wish they were both human. Catch rose up from the ground and walked past her into the house again. When she got inside Catch waved his hands to the candles and they increased in size. He gestured her to sit on the floor in the living room. Kissa kneeled down, felt his big strong hands massaging her shoulders and back. It felt like a kiss good-night and almost immediately she fell into a deep sleep.

Kissa was falling through the sky and fell to the ground. The young girl got up and looked around to see her people fighting vampires. It was a losing battle because these creatures were killing them, one by one, and they were the last humans in the land, but she didn't care about that. She looked at her arms and hands to see they were peach color and realized she was human, wearing a night gown for bed.

She walked to her parent's cottage and stepped inside to see it was lit up with candles and Catch was in the living room. He was the same age as she remembered and he was looking at her sadly. Kissa smelled his scent and couldn't help herself.

She charged after him and they began kissing and touching each other. For what seemed hours she lied on the bed and he looked at her from above while his wings spread apart like an eagle. She touched his muscular chest as he leaned towards her and his silver, blonde like hair fell onto her breasts.

"Kissa, I want to make love to you. Can I make love to you?" he whispered.

Kissa looked at the angel and was hesitant because she could feel his energy soar through her body. She had never made love to an angel before and it was scary because she was a virgin when she became a vampire

"Yes," she answered adamantly.

Catch smiled and began taking Kissa's clothes off slowly to touch her smooth legs and then her breasts. After long hours of moaning and gasping she was still hungry for sex and his blood, the essense of life that course through her body that enabled her to live forever. She was on top of him and bit his neck, when suddenly she heard him cry like a baby deer. She was hungry for love, maybe even starving for it, and would devour it like a black widow spider catching a fly.

Before Kissa knew it, she ripped large chunks of flesh from the angel's body. She rose her head up and realized that the angel's odor was really strong and he had no flesh. It was like eating a big, juicy, apple and she remembered the dream before.

The human girl could see the inside of his skin was white, but there was no apple core. She completely satisfied her needs and ate every part of the angel until he was completely gone.

She then heard a knock at the door and opened it to see vampires looking at her and bodies of dead humans rising from the ground as vampires. Tears welled in Kissa's eyes as she cried for the loss of her kin and the vampires licked their lips as they charged inside. Kissa felt every vampire get inside her body and mind until she became like them.

Kissa woke up with a gasp, to see the angel sitting cross legged with both arms out. She saw white balls of light hovering above Catch's hands and he was making the sound of a pigeon. She watched streaks of light move from the center of his chest to his wings.

Each time they shifted, his clothes disappeared and she could see his body mature. His hair began to grow shorter, but remained the same color and now he was about seventeen years of age. He opened his eyes and the process stopped.

He was bare chested and wore a gold tunic. Kissa felt sore all over her body and the last thing she remembered was getting a massage from him. Catch looked at her, smiled and nodded. She also noticed all the plants were growing wild and her flowers were blooming.

"Are you healing yourself?" Kissa asked as she watched Catch shake his head and pointed at her.

"You're healing me?" she asked and then he nodded.

Kissa started to giggle and looked out the window to see there was a tiny bit of light from the sun that was eclypsed by the moon. It was morning now and she groaned when she heard the horn blow, "I've got to go, stay here."

Kissa walked to the village square where the horned had blown to summon the vampires to a meeting with their leader Kaveezeer. Kissa looked around at the crowds of vampires and looked ahead to a plank platform where Kaveezeer stood on with his warriors and waited to hear the leader of the vampires had to say. It felt like the same old speech as yesterday until she felt something was different. The vampires near her were sniffing her and the leader looked at her strangely. He suddenly smiled at her, but then continued his attention to his fellow vampires like a king.

"We have an intruder in our village and somebody is keeping it all for themselves," said Kaveezeer smiling to all the vampires.

"I would like to take this minute to invite Kissa to stand with me," he said with a smile.

Ten warrior vampires with swords walked up and escorted her to Kaveezeer. She felt butterflies in her stomach and was scared because she thought he was going to kill her in front of the other vampires.

Once she was face to face with the leader of the village he looked at her with his hungry eyes, "tell us what is that smell?"

"I don't know what you're talking about," she stammered.

"It smells like lilacs, honey, apples and sugar, similar to how humans smell except much stronger," he smiled.

"I think I've fallen ill, I haven't fed on my goat's blood and need to do so now."

"Very well, go and drink. Don't let this meeting upset your appetite," he smiled.

Kissa walked past the warriors and was almost out of the town square when she felt like everyone was staring at her. She turned around to see Kaveezeer watching her along with every vampire.

She quickly ran inside her home and slammed the door. She took a deep breath with her eyes closed while feeling the anxiety sweep her body. Kissa opened her eyes to see the inside of her home was dark and then the angel's body illuminated. His light was so intense that it stuck to the walls and furniture, turning everything into a strange white light. The candles were lit with a silver flame and she could see the angel was very muscular and a foot taller than her. They both suddenly heard the door pounding and jerking to get open. Kissa looked outside through the window to see an endless number of vampires outside.

"You have to leave they'll kill you!" she exclaimed.

The archangel ignored her and as he moved Kissa aside and began to glow into a brighter white color. He thrust the door open with his arm and she saw him pull a sword from its sheath near his white tunic.

All the vampires in the town snarled at him and his wings opened apart. His right wing with the cast broke apart to reveal that it healed.

Catch looked at the warrior vampires who were charging after him with swords and spears, but Catch raised his sword in the air. He battled ten warriors at a time with such grace and speed that it was unbelievable, he never lost momentum after slaying each one. He used an unimaginable power to blind some of the other warriors, momentarily, with light and killed them with his sword. One warrior charged from behind and Catch spun around after splitting the vampire in front of him in half to cut the charging warrior's head off. Catch unleashed a powerful cry similar to an eagle and took on the next warrior.

Kaveezeer was charging from behind the angel with a sword and Kissa ran in front of Catch to save him. The blade slid in her chest and Catch quickly turned around. He swung his sword quickly and thrust his blade into Kaveezeer's neck, decapitating the leader of the vampires. His head rolled on the ground and started on fire.

The archangel quickly caught Kissa before she fell to the ground. Blood was slowly coming out of her mouth and Catch closed his eyes to hold back the tears.

The civilian vampires realized that they now had a chance to kill the archangel and began to close in.

What they didn't realize was that they underestimated Catche's power.

Tears began to well up in Catch's eyes as he felt his heartbeat faster, he was angry. Kissa looked up to the sky and saw a choir of angels, above her in the sky, singing in praise for love against the murky sky. She was dying and hoped that she would be able to go to that special angelic world, but she felt deep down it wasn't going to happen.

"Love is more than a feeling it's a lesson to help you on your way, but I love you Catch, I love you," she repeated, stuttering the last three words before closing her eyes.

Catch touched her face with his hand as a tear fell from his cheek onto her face. He held her close because he was emotionally hurt and looked up to the sky while his giant wings open wide. He could see the vampires closing in and let out a cry like an eagle for the angels in the sky to hear. He embraced her in his arms and set his head onto hers as his wings covered them both.

Seconds turned to minutes; light surrounded Catch and Kissa while slowly engulfing the town in a powerful light of love. After minutes went by, the light subsided, Catch got up and so did Kissa. The vampires had becom human and the town was white instead of the original dingy brown color. The archangel looked around and smiled at her and she slowly opened her eyes.

The humans looked around as they saw wolves, wear-wolves, gargoyles, eyeresettes and gothicas enter the town. The humans were scared, but then a hundred angels glided down to the town and looked at the humans. Some of the masculine archangels looked like Catch and the feminine angels looked like women. They all wore white garments or nightgowns.

It is time for the returned dominion of humans, protect them against those that would do them harm said all the archangels and angels together.

The wear-wolves, eyeresettes and gargoyles began to step inside the town to meet the humans. They were all different shapes, colors and sizes, but they were hesitant as well. Some of them had never seen a human before and didn't know what to think.

"That was your purpose? To turn me into a human girl?" asked Kissa as she looked at Catch.

Catch didn't say anything, but he lowered his eyes to the ground and then looked at her as though acknowledging her question in a slow yes.

"Stay with me, we can be together, we can make it work," she begged as she began to get emotional while her lips trembled. Catch shook his head slowly and looked sadly at her, but Kissa continued to try. "Don't you care about me? You saved my life from the vampires. I want to be with you and I know deep inside that you want to be with me," she cried and kneeled to him holding his leg and tunic. Catch looked around at the angels and the other humans, but then he realized that he couldn't leave her like this. He kneeled down to her and helped her to her feet and looked at her.

Catch looked at her for a long time and slowly smiled while taking a deep breath as he wiped her tears and shook his head slowly. She now realized why he never answered her question. He still had unfinished business elsewhere in the Ascending Realms. He loved her, but he knew that they couldn't have a normal loving relationship because he was an angel and angels fly while humans walk on the grass. Catch opened his wings and they began to move up and down. Kissa looked at

Catch and nodded her head slowly while she dried her tears with her hands. It was these loving hands that helped heal the angel's damaged wing and enabled him to fight the vampires. Catch turned his head to watch the angels take flight to the sky, *Catch, our time is done*.

Kissa jumped up and hugged him and began thinking of her dream when they made love and felt his hand over her back. She felt a burning sensation in her chest that completed her and now she understood what love was.

Catch let her go and began to take a few steps back as his wings spread apart. He turned his head to see all the humans looked emotional, watching them and were touched.

"Wait! I want to give you something," she yelled before running into the house and came back outside with a shell necklace.

"Think of me!" she said while watching Catch nod his head slowly with a smile and put the shell necklace around his neck, *I'll wear it forever*.

She smiled and watched him fly through the air to join the angels. He was gone and now a new life began as a human.

It had been five-thousand years since she was a human and everyone had to relearn everything. The humans had forgotten who they were when they were turned into vampires and the memories were not coming back as easily as others. The humans enjoyed the company of the wear-wolves, eyeresettes gothicas and gargoyles who were kind to them.

Two months went by and Kissa couldn't stop thinking about Catch. His smell was all over the house and the white light had left when he did. She was getting depressed and decided to re-decorate the home to move on with her life. She put an ad on the bulletin board at the town square for volunteers to help with the re-decorating.

Days passed until there was a knock at the door and Kissa opened it, "hi, I'm Chamberlain and I'm responding to your ad."

"Hi, I'm Kissa," she replied and invited him in."

The man had blonde hair, plain clothes and blue eyes with a striking resemblance to Catch. He looked at her a little strange because he felt uncomfortable with her staring at him.

"Is everything ok?" he asked.

"Uh yeah of course, I'm sorry would you like to have some tea?" she asked.

"I would love some," he answered and smiled the same way Catch smiled.

"Do you like sea shells?" she asked while closing the door.

www.ingramcontent.com/pod-product-compliance
Lightning Source LLC
Chambersburg PA
CBHW070222030726
47505CB00006B/1787